W9-CHB-758

He Said Together

The Lost Corisis

Book 3

Ruth Cardello

Author Contact

website: RuthCardello.com

email: ruthcardello@gmail.com

Facebook: Author Ruth Cardello

Twitter: RuthieCardello

Goodreads

goodreads.com/author/show/4820876.Ruth_Cardello

Bookbub

bookbub.com/authors/ruth-cardello

Copyright

Print Edition

ISBN eBook: 978-1-951888-28-2
ISBN Print: 978-1-951888-29-9

An original work of Ruth Cardello, 2022

He Said Together

Kal has always done whatever was necessary to protect and care for his family—even if that meant dancing for money. He's not happy with his life or himself, but what matters most are the people he loves.

The best part of Jade's bachelorette party is Kal's stripping on the stage. The worst is discovering that her fiancé is sleeping with one of the bridesmaids. Drunk and ditched by her bridal party, Jade finds comfort and encouragement from the unlikeliest of men.

When Kal suddenly finds himself financially free, he seeks out the woman he hasn't been able to forget. Their reunion is hot and heavy, but poorly timed. Jade is on the rebound and Kal's life is upside down.

He said together, but is that even possible?

Dedication

This book is dedicated to my friend Jessica. Thank you for not only inspiring me, but also my children. You're firmly planted in my heart.

CHAPTER ONE

(Months before *He Said Never*)

Jade

"A NOTHER ROUND OF shots?" Leslie, my soon-to-be sister-in-law, asked as she flagged the bartender.

I checked if my tiara was crooked before answering. "Sure." I could use the courage it might bring. The lights had dimmed around all but a stage in the middle of the room. Lights began to flicker along the long runway that led from a curtained area to the stage.

"Smile, Jade. This is your bachelorette party. Loosen up for once," Debra, Leslie's best friend, said in a tone she probably thought took the sting out of her words, but it didn't. She'd never liked me, but since Leslie had organized the trip, I didn't feel I could say no to her presence.

"I'm having fun," I lied as the waiter appeared again with drinks for all of us. When my fiancé, Robert, had suggested we celebrate in Vegas before the wedding, I knew neither of my closest friends, Sasha and Nikki, would be able to make it. Sasha was pregnant and all of her money was earmarked for the house she and her husband were saving for. Nikki was pouring all of her money into a post-graduate degree. Both had said they completely understood why I felt I had to agree to the trip.

Although Robert and I were good together, my relationship with his family was rocky. His mother thought he should have chosen someone from a better family. Once, when we'd first started dating, she'd even said as much to my face. I never told Robert because I didn't want him to argue with his mother about me. One of the first things that had attracted me to Robert was how close he was to his family.

They were the classic, picture-perfect, two-parent two-child, middle-class family. Robert's family manufactured fill valves for toilets. One day Robert would take on running that company and his dream was to have the same life his father had—with me by his side.

It was a beautiful dream and one I'd said yes to. My childhood had been full of uncertainties. I craved what life with Robert promised . . . stability, security, a home full of love and laughter.

All I had to do was learn to like the people around him. How hard could that be? I forced a smile. "Where is Daphne tonight?"

"She's not feeling well, said she had too much fun last night." Leslie shrugged and held up her glass. "She's missing out. Do you know how difficult it was to get tickets for tonight? Invio's shows are always sold out." She made a toast. "To the best show we'll all have to deny we enjoyed."

"Invio?" I downed my shot after she and Debra did, then coughed at the burn.

"The headliner? The reason a ticket to this place costs as much as some people's cars." Debra rolled her eyes then leaned toward me. "Are you really that naïve or is it an act? If I didn't know you're fucking Rob, I'd swear you're a virgin."

A few nasty retorts came to mind, but I held them back. I hadn't agreed to Vegas so we could fight. I was marrying Robert in two weeks. These people would be part of my life with him. What we needed was to find common ground. If that meant drinking with them and pretending to be excited about seeing men strip and grab themselves on stage, that's what I'd do. Deciding it was best to ignore Debra's comment, I said, "Invio. That doesn't sound like a stripper's name."

Leslie cackled loud enough to confirm that she'd already had too much to drink. "He's not just any stripper. He's *untouchable*."

Debra nodded and her lips twisted in a smile. "It's true. The men who come out before him will work the room and if you have a little cash all you have to do is nod and they'll come over . . . for whatever. He won't. He stays on the stage. They say he can't be bought and that more than one woman with money has tried." She exchanged a look with Leslie. "When you see him, you'll understand. If I didn't think my father would kill me for it, I'd trade some of my trust funds for a few minutes alone with Invio."

"Let's hope it would take more than a few minutes," Leslie joked.

I laughed along.

The lights flickered then a buff man in a tuxedo came onto the stage. I expected his intro to sound something like one to a monster truck event, but he spoke in a low, cultured tone. The room filled with anticipation. I looked around and recognized more than one person in the crowd from television. Men in suits and women in expensive dresses, all too sophisticated to do more than clap.

When the first act came out, the stage filled with six men in cowboy hats, plaid shirts, and jeans. Each was above average as far as looks and impressively muscular. I felt a little guilty as I watched them shed their shirts.

I wasn't a virgin, but what Debra sensed in me was that I'd been brought up in a very conservative household by grandparents who prayed every day I wouldn't end up like my mother. I'd done my best not to.

They wouldn't approve of this, but there isn't much they do approve of. Debra's right, I need to loosen up.

I blinked a few times quickly when the men shed their jeans in a way that revealed they were designed to come off with one good tug. I swallowed hard and tried to look more comfortable than I felt.

As the music played some of the men jumped off the stage and made their way from table to table, gyrating for the pleasure of both the men and women. This was a high-class version of scenes I'd seen in movies. The bills were large, the prompts were subtle, and the graphic nature of the moves was off the charts.

When I'm uncomfortable I often withdraw to the analytical side of my mind. First, I clarified to myself there was nothing wrong with just looking. Then I came up with scenarios for the people I saw interacting with the male dancers.

An unsmiling man paid for one of the dancers to practically mimic having sex with his scantily dressed, much younger companion. I wondered if the steamy exchange was for him, her, or both. Did it add fire to their sex life or was it compensation for an inability to please her? Either way, I couldn't look away.

Robert was a Saturday morning sex guy. Weeknights were for working late or going to the gym. Sundays were for family and catching up on work. We had a perfectly good sex life . . . better than whatever that couple had. Exciting was overrated.

It could have been the rounds of shots that kept coming to our table, but by the third or fourth act I was beginning to enjoy the show. Leslie tried to get me to interact with one of the dancers, but I refused. Still, I wouldn't say it was difficult to sit and watch attractive men bare almost everything over and over for us.

There was a pause between acts, and I could feel a hum of excitement wash over the audience. The lights dimmed again, and a man walked out dressed in dark slacks and a dark T-shirt he filled out like he'd been poured into them.

He wasn't necessarily bigger than the men who'd performed before him, but he had a presence that brought silence to the room. Jet-black hair, angry steel-gray eyes, and a body that was sheer perfection.

Unlike the others, he wasn't there to seduce or tempt. Loud music pounded the room while he walked the stage like a panther claiming his territory. His moves were powerful, athletic, and deliberate.

When he did a flip, it was executed with acrobatic precision and beauty. His landing brought him to a crouched position on one arm. When he thrust his hips toward the floor beneath him, I wasn't the only woman in the crowd who gasped.

He scanned the room with a cold contempt, then rose to his full height and shed his shirt in one powerful move that sent licks of desire shooting through me. *Robert who?*

Very slowly, he did another flip then sank down to the floor in a split while arching his back and moving his hips up and down with a rhythm that made it nearly impossible for me to catch my breath.

Like the men before him, he was simulating sex with the audience, but his was an angry fuck—so passionate and consuming there was no escape. Refusal wasn't an option.

His slacks came off last. No colorful thong for him. No, his larger than normal package was restrained by black boxer briefs that should have been less sexy since they covered more but had the opposite effect. He was a man who played by his own rules, bent to no one, and would dominate if given the chance.

My phone vibrated with a message, but I ignored it. Even if that was Robert . . . especially if that was Robert . . . it was better for me not to talk to anyone right then. I was turned on beyond the point of guilt and afraid that might come across in my voice. My only consolation was the fact that everyone around me looked like they felt the same.

No one spoke while he danced. No one moved.

We were his for the taking.

He had to have martial arts training . . . and maybe ballet? By the time his act finished I was convinced the devil himself had taught him how to lead a soul astray. I didn't know if I would have refused an intimate dance had he offered me one. My body was humming for his in a way it never had for Robert.

Scary, but I told myself that was the point of such a show.

When he left the stage, the lights came back on, and a collective release of tension was expressed in laughter and clapping.

"And that, my friends, is why Invio always sells out," Leslie said.

"How do I fuck Bradley after that?" Debra joked.

"With your eyes closed and a prayer that you don't call

out the wrong name," Leslie countered.

"That was so good I feel a little bad," I said.

They both nodded and smiled. Of all the things to connect over . . .

My phone vibrated with another message. I took my phone out. *Robert.*

Where are you? Leslie doesn't like Jade enough to hang out with her after the show. We don't have a lot of time.

The next message was a photo of Robert naked on a bed with his cock in his hand along with the following text: **Don't make me start without you.**

I had to read the texts twice before I understood that they weren't meant for me and a cold descended on me. With the photo of Robert still on my phone I raised my gaze to meet Leslie's. "Where did you say Daphne was?"

"Back at the hotel."

I held up my phone to show her what Robert had sent me. "Is there something I should know?"

"Shit," Leslie said with less shock than would have been comforting. "He told me it was over."

"Over?" I blinked through waves of shock. "I didn't know they'd ever been together. He told me she was your friend."

Debra bent to see the photo then laughed. "Once a dog always a dog. That's why I'm not with him anymore."

Wait. What? "You were with Robert?"

"He's a smooth talker, but I saw through him pretty quickly." The expression in Debra's eyes was almost sympathetic. "He doesn't belong to a gym. Wake up, Jade, he doesn't try very hard to cover his cheating." She exchanged a look with Leslie. "Honestly, I'm glad she found out. It was getting painful to watch her believe his lies."

The room spun around me. "You—you could have said something." I turned to Leslie. "Why wouldn't you tell me?"

Her eyes held no warmth for me. "What my brother does is none of my business." She stood. "Come on, Debra, I did not sign up for the drama that is about to play out. What do you say we fly back to Boston tonight?"

Debra rose to her feet. "I'm in."

Too drunk to know what to do with the anger flooding in, I stood and swayed as I said, "I should go as well—"

Her laugh cut me short. "Not with us, honey. You got yourself into this, you get yourself home. I feel for you, but my mother called it early . . . you don't exactly fit in with us."

"Thank God," I said in a hoarse voice.

"Bitch," Leslie said as she turned to walk away. "Come on, Debra."

Debra paused and gave me a pained look. "Hey, better to find out now than after you changed your name, right?"

I sank back into my seat after they left and reread the message. My eyes filled with tears that spilled down my cheeks. Had I somehow brought this on myself by fantasizing about being with the headliner? Instant bad karma?

I shook my head and the room spun again. Robert didn't

belong to a gym? All those times he'd said he was going to work out . . . Oh, my God.

I sat there going over every conversation we'd had, every lie I'd failed to recognize. Lost in my thoughts, I didn't notice that the room had begun to clear after the show had ended. Our waiter appeared with the drink bill that neither Leslie nor Debra had paid before leaving. I dug through my purse for my credit card but couldn't immediately find my wallet.

I paused, asked the waiter if he could come back in a few minutes, and burst into tears.

CHAPTER TWO

Kal

N EVER ONE TO hang after a show, I'd already changed and was headed toward the exit when I heard the bartender say, "Marcus, we've got a problem. There's a lady out there who doesn't appear to have the money to pay her tab."

"Have security handle it," the club manager answered without missing a beat.

I started to walk past them, but something in the bartender's voice brought me to a halt. "I don't feel right doing that. She's already crying and—"

"Not my problem," Marcus said impatiently.

Not mine either. Still, something held me there. I had to know. "It's not that little bachelorette with the tiara, is it?" She'd caught my eye in a way no woman who belonged to another man should.

The bartender turned to include me in the conversation. "That's her. You know her?"

"No." And it was better if it stayed that way. "What about her friends? They don't have any money either?" That wasn't how they'd come across. Working in high-end clubs had introduced me to their type on a regular basis—new money with a need to flaunt what they had. Those people didn't dine and dash.

"They left without her. I wasn't close enough to hear what they were saying, but it didn't look pretty at the end. Who leaves a drunk bride behind?"

Definitely a situation I'd be better off steering clear of. It was that last part, however, that brought out the protective side of me. The world was full of predators who lurked around, waiting for just such an opportunity. "I'll handle it."

Marcus's attention snapped to me. "*You'll* handle it?"

A lot of people backed down when Marcus questioned them in that tone, but he needed me a hell of a lot more than I needed him, and he knew it. I didn't take jobs without looking into the place. Marcus might have one of the most exclusive male revues in the country, but he'd been hurting to fill the seats before I'd signed on for a three-month gig. I didn't work for tips or without a solid contract. He couldn't touch me.

Still, the best answer in this case was the simple truth. "I have a sister. I know what I'd want someone to do for her in that case."

The bartender cautioned, "The tab is a hefty one."

I looked from him back to Marcus. "That part is not my problem and out of courtesy I'd expect it to go away."

Marcus looked a little smug at that. "You'll owe me

one."

I leaned in until we were nose to nose. "I don't owe anything to anyone. Never have, never will."

Marcus took a step back and I almost smiled. I'd been told I was paid differently than other dancers because my act was unique. It wasn't an act.

I hated dancing for money, but not my reason for doing it. The money was good and allowed me to help my mother afford treatment beyond what her insurance covered. It wouldn't always be like this. The doctors said one more back surgery and her pain would be alleviated. After that, I'd save enough to move her and my sister, Riley, into a better neighborhood. Only then would I allow myself to circle back to what I wanted—and that was to get off the stage, reenroll in college, and return my life to how it had been before my mother had told me the truth about how she'd hurt her back.

If he wasn't already dead, I would have hunted down my bio-father and killed him for what he'd done to her. She endured decades of fear and pain all because of one man— Antonio. The name alone was enough to turn my stomach.

I couldn't go back in time and change what had happened to her, but I could ensure she received the best medical treatments out there. That wasn't cheap. Dropping out of college to make that happen had been a necessity— and dancing paid better than any of the jobs I'd been able to find. Riley had left college to help as well, but I carried the bulk of the financial weight. I'd do much worse than baring skin for strangers before I'd ever let my sister do anything similar. She worked in a T-shirt shop for her best friend and played bridesmaid at weddings for extra cash. Although we'd shared the same womb, Riley and I were very different people. Like our mother, she'd been born with a sweet, optimistic nature.

I was cursed with a darker side, a demon I barely kept in check. It was that rage that I put on stage each night.

And women loved it.

How anyone could find the anger I had for the "sperm donor"—the man who had beaten my mother so badly that she'd nearly miscarried me and Riley—attractive was beyond me.

He'd broken her back, left her in constant pain and fear, and never looked back. Yet somehow, she'd given Riley and me a loving home and a somewhat normal childhood. She deserved every good thing we could do for her.

I shook my head as I imagined what my fans would think if they knew she was the reason I was on stage. They'd disperse for sure. Invio was a bastard they loved to imagine taming and it was best to let them maintain that fantasy.

The bartender shifted from one foot to another. "What should I do with the tab?"

I looked Marcus in the eye and let the demon in me meet him there. He blinked first. "Comp the drinks."

I nodded once and turned my attention to the reason I

wasn't already back in my hotel room. The little brunette was the only person left in the main room. She was slumped forward, face hidden in her hands, with her tiara hanging precariously off one side of her head. I sat in the seat across from her. "On a scale of one to ten how drunk are you?"

From behind her hands she mumbled, "Nine. Maybe twelve." She lowered her hands revealing a face smudged with makeup. "I forgot my wallet at the hotel." She blinked a few times quickly. "I could come back with money."

"The tab is paid. Do you have anyone who can come for you?"

Fresh tears filled her eyes and her face crumpled. "I did, but he's fucking Daphne." She turned her phone toward me and tapped the screen.

I read the messages, glanced at the photo he'd sent, and grimaced. "What a douche."

She waved her hands in the air. "We're getting—*were* getting married in two weeks. Now what do I do? Why would he do this?" She picked up her phone. "I need to ask him why."

I removed the phone from her hands and replaced it on the table between us. "You don't. He'll only lie. I know it doesn't feel this way now, but he did you a favor."

Her gaze met mine and for a moment her pain was so tangible I felt it. "Favor? He was my chance to have the life I've always wanted."

I remembered something my mother had said once about

how she'd initially believed my bio-father was her "Prince Charming." He'd swept in, said all the right things, and sold her a fantasy about how perfect life would be with him. "He wasn't. I don't know what he told you, but the man who sent you those texts doesn't give a shit about you." She burst into tears again and I swore. I probably could have worded that better. I rubbed a hand over my forehead and tried again. "Don't cry. He's not worth it."

She sucked in a shaky breath. "We were going to have a nice house, some kids, and live happily ever after."

I cocked my head to one side, intrigued by something that was none of my business. "Do you even love him?"

"Of course I do."

"I don't think you do."

She glared at me. "I don't care what you think. You don't know me or him."

"I'm not saying what he did wasn't a dick move, it's just interesting that you sound more upset about not getting that house and kids than losing him."

If looks could kill I would have been dead. "Why are you here? Shouldn't you be *dancing* somewhere?"

My eyebrows shot up. "Ouch. Tell me what you really think of me."

She looked away and blushed and my heart began to thud in my chest. There was definitely something there, but neither of us were in a place to act on it. In a quiet voice, she said, "Sorry, I'm just angry and hurt and disappointed . . .

mostly in myself. I can't believe I was so stupid. If he really was at the gym a few nights a week he'd have a much better body."

I smiled at that and removed her tiara. "That's better. Mr. Pudgy doesn't deserve you."

She sniffed and wiped at the corners of her eyes. "He isn't fat—just soft."

I didn't see how that was better. "Okay."

She sniffed again and raised her gaze to mine. "I liked who I was when I was with him. We had dinner parties with friends. My grandparents liked him. Outside of my degree, he was the first thing I've done that they really approved of. They want to see me settled and safe. With him, I would have been."

I didn't like that she considered her life unsafe without a man. What did she feel she needed to be saved from? "Are you in some kind of trouble?"

She laughed without humor. "No. I'm my own trouble. I don't blame them for wanting me to do better than my mother did. They feel like they failed her and they're trying to do better with me."

She didn't look like someone who'd done worse than putting trust in the wrong person. "What happened to your mother?"

Her face crumpled again. "She overdosed when I was a baby. I never knew her."

"So your grandparents raised you?"

"Yes."

"And they think marrying a nice guy will keep you from becoming your mother, and you want to make them proud?"

She took an audible breath. "I don't know. I guess."

I laid my hand over hers. "You don't need him. You don't need anyone. You'll feel a lot better when you free yourself from the belief that you're not enough on your own. You are."

Her breathing slowed as she calmed. "I don't need him."

"Exactly."

"I have a job. I can support myself. I don't do drugs or even drink—except tonight." She brought a hand to her temple. "My head is spinning."

"Where are you staying?"

"At the Bellagio."

"I'll call a car for you."

"I can do it. I have the app." Tears filled her eyes again. "You're right, I don't need anyone."

I nodded and removed my hand from hers. "You got this."

Her phone rang. She checked the caller but didn't answer. "It's Robert. I don't want to talk to him."

"Then don't."

She waved the phone between us. "I should say something."

"Allow me." I held out my hand for the phone. She handed it over, I typed **Fuck off** then hit send.

When I handed the phone back to her, she smiled sadly. "You read my mind." Her phone vibrated with another message. She shook her head while reading it. "He wants to know where I am. He says he can explain." She typed something back then raised her gaze back to meet mine. "I told him we can talk tomorrow. He's not happy."

I didn't like that. Nope, not at all. "What did he say?"

"He said he's coming over. He thinks I'm back at my room."

"Tell him no."

"I did. He said he's coming anyway."

"Tell him you're not alone."

Her eyes flew to mine. "What?"

"You're drunk. He's angry. Men have been known to do some pretty ugly things when they think they can. Don't give him the chance to."

Her mouth rounded. "He'll be even more upset if I tell him I'm with someone."

"As upset as you were when you found out he was fucking Daphne?"

"You're right. We're over." She texted something else to him. "I told him I'm still here and with someone." She frowned. "He said he's going to come here."

"Do you want him to?"

Her answer was immediate. "No."

"Give me the phone."

She hesitated then handed her phone to me again.

"What's your name?" I asked.

"Jade," she said barely above a whisper.

Jade. Nice name. It fit her.

I wrote: **Kal here. Jade is with me tonight. Call her tomorrow if you'd like. She might still remember your name, but probably not.** Just to piss the douche off I took a quick selfie and sent it along with the text.

I handed the phone back. Her eyes rounded. "Thank you—I think. I'm not with you though. I mean, we're talking, but—"

"Don't worry, I don't mix business and pleasure. All I want is to know that you're safe."

She searched my face. "How do I know I can trust you?"

It was a good question. She had no reason to. I took out my phone and dialed someone who always knew what to say to make a situation better. She picked up on the second ring, "Kal? Is everything okay?"

"Yes, Mom, everything is fine. I'm here with a woman who had a little bit too much to drink and just broke up with her fiancé because she caught him cheating. I offered to take her home and she's understandably worried that my intentions might not be honorable."

"Oh, that's horrible. Do I know her?"

"No, we just met. I'd put her in cab alone but that's not safe in her condition."

"Let me talk to her."

I handed the phone to Jade. She looked around at first as

if she didn't believe what she was hearing, then she met my gaze again as she spoke. "I know. He said the same." She blushed. "I came with friends, well, not really friends, to see his show for my bachelorette party." She looked away as she added, "It was very nice." Then in response to something my mother must have asked, she said, "They left me."

She slurred her words as she told my mother about how she'd come to be drunk and alone at the club. As they spoke, I had the opportunity to appreciate the little hand moves Jade made when she was nervous. She was delicately built with the most beautiful eyes I'd ever looked into. I told myself not to imagine the two of us intimately entwined, but once I let that thought in it was difficult to dispel.

A few minutes later, Jade handed the phone back to me. "She wants to speak to you again."

I held the phone to my ear. "Mom?"

"You're doing the right thing, Kal. Take that girl home and make sure she's safe then call me."

"That was the plan."

"I love you."

"Love you too." I ended the call and repocketed my phone. "The next move is up to you, Jade. Are you okay with me going with you to make sure you make it back to your hotel?"

She took a moment to answer. "Your mother said she raised you to be a gentleman."

"She did."

She pointed to the room around us in a circle. "Then why this . . ."

My voice held some growl. "We all do what we have to do." I looked around. The staff was waiting for us to leave.

When I looked back into Jade's eyes, she seemed conflicted. "I don't need anyone to take me home."

"But?"

"I know I'll be fine. I can handle talking to Robert—tomorrow. Right now, I'm so . . . confused. I shouldn't have done those last shots. I could close my eyes right now and nap here. I want to tell you I don't need help, but maybe I do."

I rose to my feet and held out my hand to her. "We've all been in that place. Let's get you home."

She placed her hand in mine and stood. I didn't let myself linger on how good that innocent touch felt. We weren't going there.

CHAPTER THREE

Jade

S EATED IN THE back of a hired car, I tried to tell myself it was the alcohol that had me confused, but it also had something to do with the mountain of masculinity seated mere inches from me. How was it possible that feeling shredded by Robert's betrayal didn't stop my heart from racing every time Invio looked at me?

"Invio—"

"Kal. My name is Kal Ragsdale."

"Really? That sounds so . . . normal."

His smile lit up the night. "I *am* normal."

I had no filter at that point, so I said, "But on stage you were so angry . . . so . . ."

His expression dimmed a little. "I'm that too."

I fell silent as a wave of nausea came and passed. I tried my best to sound sober. "Thank you for helping me out tonight. I'm sure you weren't looking to get involved in my mess."

"I wasn't, but it's not a big deal."

"It is to me." There was a pain in his eyes that reached

past my inebriation to pull at my heart. "What you said earlier about men doing ugly things when they think they can . . ."

He inhaled audibly and looked straight forward as he said, "My mother. Twenty-six years later and she's still healing from his abuse." There was a fire in his eyes when his gaze met mine again. "I have no tolerance for men who mistreat women."

Neither of us said anything for a long moment. His words hung in the air between us. "I'm sorry."

"Not your fault." His expression tightened. "She's fine now, but don't make the same mistakes she did. Don't trust someone so much that you make yourself vulnerable to them. And if someone raises a hand to you, you fight—fight them so hard they don't dare ever try it again." He looked away. "I try to understand why my mother didn't, but I don't. She believes she deserved what he did to her. She didn't. No one does."

In a move meant to comfort him, I placed a hand on his thigh.

There was sheer torment in his eyes when he growled, "Don't."

I removed my hand. "Sorry, I was just—"

He leaned closer. "And don't apologize. Don't give me that power."

I swallowed hard. "I don't understand."

"I'm no hero." His breath was hot on my cheek and his

mouth hovered over mine. "You're beautiful and I'm tempted, but that doesn't mean anything will happen between us. It does mean, though, that you should keep your hands to yourself."

My breath caught in my throat, and I'd never been more turned on. Right or wrong, there was no denying the heat washing through me in waves. Every inch of me was painfully aware of every inch of him. "Because you're tempted?" The words flew out before I had time to ask myself if they should.

He gave me a long look. "You've had too much to drink and you're hurting. It's natural to not want to be alone. Some guys would take advantage of that. I won't."

His assessment of how I felt was spot-on and left me feeling exposed. "No, because you're so much better than other guys. Mr. Perfect is that what you want me to believe?"

His laugh was more of a bark. "Far from it." Then his expression turned more serious again. "I'm human, just like you. I've done some shit I regret, spent time asking myself if I was doing anything right . . . but I get up each morning and try to do better. That's all I'm doing, just trying to do a little better each day."

Swoon. "You have a beautiful soul, Kal Ragsdale."

He tapped a finger on the tip of my nose and said, "And your judgement is impaired, but I'll take the compliment anyway."

It was definitely the alcohol . . . I have no other justification for why I said, "I *am* hurting and you're right, I don't want to be alone tonight."

"All I'm doing is dropping you at the door of your hotel."

I shook my head and yawned. "I know." His shoulder looked so tempting. What would he do if I rested my head there . . . just for a minute? I scooted closer, laid my head on his shoulder, and the last thing I heard before I passed out was him swearing.

I woke a short time later to Kal urging me to get out of the car so he could walk me to my room. I climbed out and swayed. He steadied me with an arm around my waist and led me into the hotel lobby.

"I'll walk you to your room door," he said in a gruff tone.

I pulled slightly away from him. "You don't have to. I'm fine." Then I tripped and would have faceplanted on the floor of the lobby if he hadn't caught me and hauled me back to his side.

"I'd do it for anyone. What floor are you on?"

I told him as we made our way to the elevator. "I have my own room because his sister and her friends don't really like me, and Robert said we should stay at different hotels." I came to an abrupt halt as that suddenly made sense. "So I wouldn't notice that he and Daphne were fucking."

He brought a finger to my lips briefly. "Shhh. Not everyone in the hotel needs to know that."

I looked around, noticed people watching us, and felt belligerent rather than embarrassed. "His name is Robert Bouchard," I told the crowd. "Only date him if you want to find out he's screwing someone else two weeks before you marry him."

Kal dipped his head down to mine. "Feel better now?"

I didn't so I threw an arm up in the air and loudly proclaimed, "He's not even that good in bed. I was willing to settle for that."

"Never settle," a woman from across the lobby called out. "Not even if he looks as good as your guy does."

"What a shame," someone else called out, "to be that hot and not good in bed."

Kal straightened at my side and announced, "I'm *not* Robert Bouchard."

"Thank God," the first woman said and there was a general round of laughter.

I gave Kal's wide chest a pat. "This is Kal." I looked up at him and smiled. "He's a good guy. He rescued me tonight."

A beautiful woman in a short, tight dress walked by and said, "You can rescue me anytime, Kal. In fact, if your little friend passes out, you can rescue me tonight. I'll wait for you down in the bar."

I made a growl deep in my chest and tried to tell her he was mine, but my words jumbled into gibberish.

"I appreciate the offer," Kal said smoothly, "but I've got all I can handle right here." With that he turned me toward the elevator again and ushered me there.

We weren't alone in the elevator, but that didn't stop me from saying, "I'm sorry. I know you're not mine."

He looked down at me and gave me a little squeeze. "You probably won't remember any of this tomorrow, so don't sweat it."

I tapped my temple. "I won't forget it. I have a really good memory. Some say porno—no, photographic. Photographic memory. That's how I did so well in school. I can remember everything I read." My slipup tickled my imagination. "What would a pornographic memory even be? Would I only remember naughty videos?" I giggled at the thought of what kind of degree a person would get with that skill. That was followed by another thought I couldn't contain. "I must have that skill because I won't forget a moment of you on stage. When you hovered just above the floor . . . I felt like you were dancing for me. Every woman did. That's a gift."

Kal groaned. The elevator opened at my floor, and he led me out of it, down the hall, and to the door of my room. "Do you have your key?"

"I do," I said without looking for it. He had the most incredible jaw. So strong. So smooth. I wanted to touch it. I raised my hand to, but he caught it in his and brought my hand back to my side.

"Find your key or give me your purse and I will."

"Right. My key." I dug it out.

He opened the door to my room with it then handed it back to me. I took a step inside the room then turned and replaced my key in my purse. That was when I noticed my phone and part of our earlier conversation came back to me. "Do you really think Robert would hurt me?"

Kal pocketed his hands and shrugged. "I don't know."

"He's never hit me."

"That's a good thing."

"I shouldn't be afraid of him. He cheated on me, but he's never hurt me."

"Then you're fine."

I didn't feel fine. "Why am I afraid to be alone right now?"

Kal hung his head. "I did that. I planted that thought in your head. I shouldn't have. That's my issue, not yours."

It wasn't enough. "What if he comes here after you leave?"

"Bolt your door. You're safe. And tomorrow you'll remember that."

It was hard to let him go, harder than it should have been. A man like him was probably with a different woman every night. Still, I wanted to have a piece of him to hold onto. "Tell me something you don't tell anyone else."

He cocked his head to one side and took a moment to answer. "I wanted to be a marine biologist." He shook his head. "I will be one—someday."

I brought both hands to my chest. "I'm a marine biologist."

His smile was immediate. "You're making that up."

I crossed my heart. "No, it's true. That's what I went to school for."

"Tell me it's amazing. I've always loved scuba diving and travel. To do that while making a difference in the future of the ocean . . . Have you seen the work they're doing in coral nurseries with speeding up its growth in the Caribbean? Being part of a project like that is the dream I'm working toward."

"I love the ocean too. And scuba diving. I've always wanted to travel." I rocked back onto my heels as a deep sadness settled over me. "I haven't been anywhere, or even in the ocean, in a long time. I work for a restaurant chain maintaining their large tanks." Tears welled in my eyes. "It's so boring, but it's steady pay and Robert doesn't like the idea of me out on a boat. He hates the water."

"What he likes doesn't matter anymore." Kal took a step inside the door. "You're going to soar without him, Jade. It'll be scary at first, but you're stronger than you know."

I blinked back my tears. "My grandparents were so proud of me, but I can't live for them."

"No, you can't."

"And I don't want Robert back."

"I hope you remember that tomorrow."

"Why are you in Vegas?" I had to ask, but the answer came to me before he answered. "You're doing it for your family. You put your dream aside for them."

His eyes shone with emotion. "They would do the same for me." He cleared his throat. "And my time will come."

We stood there looking into each other's eyes and I would have sworn I glimpsed his very soul—and it was as beautiful as the rest of him. "I wish I had your confidence."

He smiled. "I wish I was half as good of a man as your booze goggles have convinced you I am." He reached out and cupped my cheek. "Tomorrow when you wake up, don't be sad about what you lost tonight . . . be relieved. You're free. You can do whatever you want to now. Go save the world."

I swayed and sniffed. No one had ever believed in me that way. My whole life I'd been told to be more careful, dream smaller, be happier with less. His words lit a fire of resolve in me. "I'm smart and now I'm free. I can do anything I want."

"Exactly." He dropped his hand. "And someone needs to keep those reefs thriving until I can get there and join the fight."

"I would love to do that."

"Then do it. Make it happen."

I nodded. "I will."

He took a step back. "I should go. Bolt the door behind me."

I reached out and touched his arm. "Will I see you again?"

He glanced down at my hand then met my gaze. "I'm planted here for another month and I'm easy enough to find on social media." He leaned in until his lips almost touched mine. "Send me a picture of you out on a boat. I'd love to hear about your new job and how you take on that challenge. I could use some good news."

"Kal Ragsdale," I repeated his name because I was afraid I might forget it.

He bent closer and ever so gently kissed me, then said, "Jade . . ."

"Tremblay," I whispered.

"Good night, Jade Tremblay."

"Good night."

He withdrew out the door, closing it behind him. I bolted it then turned and leaned against it. My eyelids felt heavy, and I could have slept again right there, but I was afraid if I went to sleep I might forget Kal, and I didn't want to.

I hunted my phone out and called Nikki. I heard the slur in my voice as I said her name when she answered.

"Having fun, I see," Nikki said with a laugh.

I sank to sit on the floor. "Not really. Robert and I are over."

"Oh, my God, what happened?"

I rubbed a hand over my eyes. The room spun and it would have been easy, too easy to let myself sink into sleep. "I need to tell you about Kal. I may be a little bit . . . okay, a lot drunk right now, but I've never felt this way about anyone before."

"Hold on, who is Kal? Is he why you and Robert are over?"

I took a deep breath and waved a hand through the air. "No, Robert is why Robert and I are over. And Daphne. But I'm pretty sure I'll remember that tomorrow. What I don't want to forget is what Kal said to me."

In response to prompting from her, I started at the beginning of the evening when I'd reluctantly agreed to have my bachelorette party at an all-male revue, with women I knew didn't like me. "It was all wrong," I said. "I see it now. I was trying to be someone I'm not. I'm free now."

"I don't understand," Nikki said.

I told her about Invio . . . Kal. I told her everything I could remember that I'd felt, what he'd said, and how much I wanted to quit my job and put my degree to real use. "He wants me to send him photos of me at my new job. Nikki, he was in school to be a marine biologist just like I am. I think I met my soul mate tonight."

"Sounds like you had quite a night," Nikki said. "Are you okay now?"

"I am." I pushed myself to my feet, made my way to the bed, then flopped onto it. "I'm never going to drink again."

She chuckled. "I don't blame you. You sound like you're going to be hurting in the morning."

I let my eyes close. "I should be hurting now. I'm not getting married, Nikki."

"I know, hon."

"But I'm not shattered—I'm free." And so tired. "I don't want to forget this feeling."

"Promise to call me in the morning."

I couldn't promise anything as I let myself drift away.

CHAPTER FOUR

Kal

I PUT JADE out of my thoughts long enough to get restless sleep that night. The next morning, I checked several accounts on my phone for a message from her, but there wasn't one. I fought the urge to return to her hotel to make sure she was okay, but I'd already become more involved than I should have.

She knew where to find me.

Knowing women, she'd already forgiven him, and they were flying back to—wherever they were from—to have that wedding she claimed was off. Men made promises. Women believed them because they wanted to. There was no protecting a person from a bad choice if they wanted to make it. In the business I was in, I unfortunately saw the reality of that on a regular basis. For male dancers, sex with a different woman was too easy to get each night. Hell, after a good enough show, too many women were open to wild romps alone or in groups. The lure of that was enough to pull even a good man into the drinking and drugs that went hand in hand with a party lifestyle.

I'd fallen into that world when I first started dancing. The more I worked out, the more women wanted me and, in the absence of anything more that made sense, being wanted had felt good.

Until it didn't. Waking up next to women I would never see again got old. Hangovers and the need for a quick high got old as well. It was after a night of dancing at a dive club, while counting the cash women had stuffed into my thong, that I said, "No." *No more.*

I didn't want to dance anymore, even if it was the only way to pay off my mother's medical bills. I didn't like who I was becoming, and I hated the reason I was there. The same man who had destroyed my mother's life was also destroying mine.

I was still angry the next night when I returned to the stage. So angry that I didn't let anyone touch me. It was the first show I'd done sober in a long time, and I started it by announcing that I was *inviolable*, unbreakable, untouchable.

When I danced that night, it wasn't for the audience, it was for me, and I didn't hold back my disgust for what I was doing. I let them see my rage.

A woman had called out, "We love you, Invio!" and my stage name was born.

So, yeah, I understood how a person could be led so far away from their dreams that they started to think they couldn't be more. I understood how trying to do the right thing could lead a person down the wrong road.

I hoped that was what Jade remembered from our encounter. If nothing else, she might find comfort in the realization that she wasn't alone. On the other hand, with how much she'd had to drink, there was a chance she might not remember me at all—not the stage me, not the real me.

Forgetting Jade wouldn't be as easy for me. It had been a long time since I'd met someone who touched me on any level beyond the physical. I wanted to hear that she'd broken free of everyone holding her back. I wanted it so badly I had to take a second look at the man in the mirror.

How much of what I wanted for her was a reflection of what I was yearning for? What was holding me back and how much was I part of my own problem?

No one enjoys asking themselves those questions but doing so led me to using my day off to fly to Catalina Island for the first dive I'd taken in nearly two years. I had to rent gear, join a group of divers to make it affordable, and fly back the same day to save myself the cost of a hotel room, but it was worth it.

Diving Farnsworth Banks wasn't for the inexperienced and I chose a dive that was led by a man who was known for championing the protection of those ecological reserves. It was a three-tank boat trip from the mainland and the waters were rough.

The tour guide was a master diver on a personal crusade to save the island's endangered hydrocoral. We tied at one of the few permanent mooring buoys. He led us along anchor lines from other boats to the bottom of the ocean so we could see firsthand the devastation at the end of the line: crushed rock, shattered purple coral, pulverized starfish, mussels, and plants. He photographed the damage and, later on the boat, shared his addiction to tracking down the names of the owners of each boat, even the super yachts. He then sent them a mock invoice along with the photos of the damage their anchor had left in its wake. The payee of the invoice? Future generations because that's who they were stealing this natural resource from. He included a QR code to a site on how to fund the initiative to install more mooring buoys to save the coral.

So far, his method had not proven effective to gain support for the project, but I understood his motivation. He dove the way I danced. Neither of us were achieving what we wanted. I didn't tell him that. I doubted he'd see the correlation. It was also refreshing to not be Invio for a day.

I returned from the trip with photos of myself exploring the damaged seabed and a desire to help Farnsworth Banks. Both quickly faded in importance as soon as I stepped back into my life. I had no one to talk to about why the trip had been important to me, no one who would find the photos more than mildly interesting.

So I danced and made money for what was important— paying off my mother's prior surgery so we could move forward with scheduling her next one.

A week later I received a package at the club.

I told myself to wait but couldn't. I tore the wrapping off and smiled when I saw the title of the book: **Save the Ocean, Save the World: Stories from the World's Leading Marine Scientists.**

There was a message inside the flap of the book: **Thank you for believing in me. I needed someone to. I'm single now, unemployed, and moving to Florida to be by the ocean. If you really do want me to send you photos of my journey, text me and we can stay in touch. Jade**

She included her phone number then added: **I can't save the world alone. Get that degree and join me.**

I blinked back a wave of emotion that nearly caused me to embarrass myself in front of my fellow dancers. The urge to drop everything and fly off to Florida was real, but I couldn't. I couldn't put what I wanted before what my family needed.

Someday. Someday it'll be my turn.

One of my fellow dancers came up to me and asked, "What'd you get?"

When I showed him the book he shrugged. "Lame. Is that from your parents?"

I shook my head and smiled. He didn't need to understand.

After the show I took the book back to my hotel room and read it until I fell asleep. I didn't text Jade that night because I didn't know what to say. I didn't text her the next day either. I wasn't ready. I booked a flight east to visit my family and remind myself where my priorities needed to remain.

I don't remember a time when my mother didn't struggle with her health, but rather than being a burden it had bonded us closely together. Riley and I had both needed to grow up faster than many did, but neither of us resented it. Our mother was one hundred percent love and support. She'd instilled in us a strong sense of family and responsibility. Hard work was simply a part of life and how one demonstrated love and loyalty.

Being home felt good. I joked that Riley still saw the world through rose-colored glasses, and she joked that I couldn't see much because my enormous ego blocked my view. To prove my humility, I flexed for them, which won a round of groans and laughter.

Teagan, Riley's best friend since childhood, joined us and it was as if no time had gone by at all. The four of us played cards, teased Mom about her cooking, and ended the evening watching movies, smushed together on a couch that was as old as Riley and I were.

And it was good—so good that I hated to leave the next day, but I had to get back for my next show. We didn't talk about my job because they respected that I didn't like to. I did enjoy hearing about Riley's escapades as a bridesmaid for hire, though. Only Riley could make a living from something like that and enjoy doing it.

Teagan had graduated top of her class from MIT only to open a print shop in our hometown. I was no one to judge, so I didn't. She didn't like to talk about her work either, but Riley worked for her part-time and the two had remained close. Most of my friends had fallen to the wayside when I'd started dancing, so in some ways, they were doing better than I was.

I returned to Vegas with renewed determination to get us all in a better place. I worked out harder and hired a choreographer who had experience with acrobatics. I already had a brand, but I needed to take it to the next level. My moves needed to do more than turn women on, they needed to gain the attention of a venue that would hire me when my current gig was over.

Over the next few weeks, I took my act to a higher athletic level and gained the attention of a talent scout. She offered me a lucrative contract to take my act internationally. I accepted because more money meant a faster track to reaching the goal of comfort for my mother and freedom for me and Riley.

When my Vegas contract ended, I flew home. In the humble kitchen that hadn't changed a bit from childhood, I handed my mother my sign-on bonus, which was nearly enough to pay off her last medical bill. She cried and said she was so proud of me. Riley was proud as well, but she had questions. I could tell it bothered her that I'd accepted the job without telling anyone. It was an uncomfortable conversation that she tried to spin into a positive light.

That was Riley.

We had a brief, awkward celebration that ended with me asking them to keep my news to themselves. Riley saved me from needing to explain why by announcing that Teagan wanted to meet us for lunch.

Never had I been so happy to visit Teagan's T-shirt shop. My relief was short-lived as soon as Riley burst through the shop door and said, "You have to tell Teagan, Kal. We should celebrate your good news."

I groaned. "You *just* promised you wouldn't say anything to anyone."

Riley waved at Teagan. "Teagan isn't just anyone—she's Teagan. Come on. If you won't tell her, let me. Please."

I folded my arms across my chest. Teagan had spent enough time at our house that she felt like another sister, but I wasn't ready for another celebration about something I wanted to put out of my head for a few days.

Teagan seemed to understand. She gave me a sympathetic smile and said, "Riley, if Kal doesn't want me to know, that's okay."

Riley was too excited to do that. I shook my head. "Never tell Riley anything. She can't keep a secret to save her life."

Teagan made a pained face. "Speaking of secrets—"

Riley spoke over her. "Oh, come on. You seriously care if Teagan knows?"

I couldn't begrudge her enthusiasm. Riley really was happy for me. We each had our own way of coping. If she needed to throw glitter on the unpleasant and celebrate to deal with it, who was I to tell her not to?

Yay, I'll be stripping internationally now.

"There's something I need to tell both of you," Teagan added.

Frustrated, I threw my hands up in the air. "Fine. Teagan, a talent scout was at my last show and offered me an international gig. Her company wants to fly me around the world. I couldn't turn down the offer—it's enough to pay off the rest of what we owe for Mom and get Riley back in school. It looks like I'm in the big leagues now."

"A headliner," Riley said with pride. "But I'm not taking the extra money. We'll talk to the hospital and see if we can get Mom's next surgery on a payment plan." She looked at me with a level of understanding only a twin could have. "I know you hate dancing, Kal, and none of this is what either of us wanted . . . but that doesn't mean you shouldn't be proud of your accomplishment. You're making more money than any of your college friends with their fancy office jobs. And we won't always be in this place. The doctor said this surgery might do the trick. We'll pay that off and then both go back to school. Who knows, maybe I'll find a job so good before that that I'll pay for you to go back before me."

She meant every word of it. I gave her a quick hug. "I'd never let that happen, but I love you for wanting to take care of me, Riley."

She smiled up at me. "I've got your back—always. After all, you're the only brother I have."

Teagan interjected, "Actually, about that . . ."

There was something in her voice that pulled my attention from Riley to her. She looked nervous when she said, "Your biological father had five children."

We all froze, and her words hung there in the silence.

I spoke first. "What are you talking about?"

"Mom said our father was dead," Riley said, looking lost.

Teagan answered in a slow, measured tone. "He is, but he was with other women before that. He's been dead for about twenty years."

His death wasn't news to me, but that he had other children was. "From the little I know about the man, I'm glad he's dead. He's the reason for our mother's pain. No offense, but I want no part of a family reunion that revolves around him."

Riley touched my arm. "Hang on, Kal. These people aren't him." She looked to Teagan. "Brothers or sisters?"

"One sister, two brothers. All older with children of their own."

"That's a lot." Riley moved to sit on one of shop's stools.

"I hear five is the perfect number," Teagan added.

Not in my mind. "We have all the family we need," I growled.

Riley directed her question to her friend. "How long have you known?"

"Not long, and at first I didn't know if it was true. Then I spoke to your mother, and she confirmed that it was."

Teagan clasped her hands together. "She made me promise not to tell you, but I didn't feel like it was something I could keep from you."

Nodding, Riley said, "I can see that. I've asked her about him over the years. Any hint of curiosity would upset her. She said he was a very dangerous person from a dangerous family. I always wondered if we were related to the mob or something like that."

"Something like that," Teagan said, then quickly added, "I mean . . . nothing like that."

I'd never wasted time wondering if we had family on our bio-father's side. I ran a hand through my hair and said, "I don't want anything to do with them."

"I don't if they're dangerous," Riley said tentatively. "Are they?"

"No." Teagan didn't look all that certain about that claim.

Riley turned to meet my gaze. "A sister and two brothers." Her mouth rounded. "I'm an aunt. You're an uncle, Kal. Maybe we should at least meet them."

Oh, hell no.

"You already have," Teagan interjected.

"When?" Riley stood. "How?"

Looking as uncomfortable with the topic as I felt, Teagan said, "Your father's name was Antonio Corisi."

His last name didn't matter to me. None of what Teagan was saying did.

Riley brought a hand up to her temple. "So Judy Corisi wasn't at the shop to design a logo for her father."

Judy Corisi. There was a famous Corisi and his daughter's name was Judy. The whole world knew who they were.

Teagan looked guilty. "No."

"Right. Dominic Corisi is our brother and the Queen of England is our aunt." No one laughed at my joke.

Teagan lifted and dropped a shoulder. "You have that half right. Antonio had two children with his wife, Rosella: Dominic and Nicole. So, yes. Dominic Corisi is your brother. Half brother if you want to be technical."

"No," I said with all the disgust that was filling me.

"Yes," Teagan said gently.

Riley waved a hand around. "That would make Judy our niece. She was there to meet me?"

"And me." Teagan added, "It's complicated and not all of it matters right now."

Riley looked confused. "You said you haven't known for long, but it sounds like you know an awful lot about them."

I wanted no part of the conversation, but I wasn't about to leave Riley alone with this. Teagan continued, "Gian is Judy's uncle. He and Dominic have the same mother, but different fathers."

"Who's Gian?" I asked, only to try to make some sense of this.

"Her boyfriend," Riley answered slowly.

I'd heard enough. "Yeah, leave me out of that clusterfuck."

Riley was getting more agitated, though. She looked at Teagan and asked, "Why didn't you say something when I brought Judy in? There I was thinking I'd landed a potential client for you, excited and going on about it like an idiot when something entirely different was going on."

"I'd promised Fara—" Teagan began to say, but Riley cut her off.

"I would have told *you*."

"I'm sorry." *She should be.*

Riley waved her off.

Teagan turned to me. "I thought I was doing the right thing."

Not good enough. This wasn't an innocent spin and spill. Loyalty was huge to me, and she'd just betrayed us. If these were the same people my mother had said she needed to stay hidden from, Teagan might well have put our family in danger. "If my mother asked you not to say anything, she had good reason to. Not that it matters now, I guess. They already know about *us*."

"They didn't for a long time. Judy and Gian thought there might be a chance Antonio had more children and their search led them here." Teagan looked so apologetic it was hard to remain angry with her. "I am so sorry. I love you both and your mother. You've been my family, sometimes even more so than my own. I don't know if I did any of this the right way, but I tried to do what I thought was best because I love you."

Riley was easier to win over than I was. She said, "We love you too. I know how you get tangled up in your head sometimes and can't get out of your own way." She paused. "Wait, did they know what happened to my mother?"

"They didn't, but they do now." Teagan checked her watch. "As of about an hour or so ago. Gian flew down to tell them."

I had to know if Teagan knew something I didn't. "Why is Mom afraid of these people?"

Teagan told us about the man who'd come to see our mother when she was in the hospital, the one who'd warned her that hiding was the only way she could protect herself and her children from Antonio. I just about threw up in my mouth. "So someone knew about us all along and did nothing to help our mother. I want nothing to do with these people."

Teagan didn't give up there. She said, "You don't have to make any decisions today. There is more to their story. Why don't we get something to eat and I'll tell you what I know?" Over sandwiches and coffee, Teagan mapped out our family, the one she wanted us to consider ours anyway, and then told us about another family—the Romanos. "The story of our family is heavy on the name Gian."

Teagan blushed. "I learned everything about your family through him."

"And she's fucking him," Riley added with a smile.

Teagan slugged her arm. "No, I'm—"

I arched an eyebrow. She definitely was.

With a grin, she conceded, "I am and it's fantastic."

Despite all the emotions raging within me, I chuckled. Maybe life wasn't supposed to make sense. "Well, okay then."

Riley clapped. "You should see them together, Kal. Talk about sizzle. I hope I meet someone who makes me feel that way someday."

"I'm happy for you, Teagan." I was. I cared about Teagan. "Just be careful. He's probably nothing like our father—" I made a face and continued, "I hate to even call him that."

"Just say Antonio," Riley suggested.

I nodded. "Gian is probably nothing like Antonio was, but people with money aren't like us. If he crosses a line, if he ever makes you feel uncomfortable—tell me. I'll handle it."

Teagan's eyes teared up. "I'm sure that won't be necessary, but thanks." After a pause. "I really like him."

Riley leaned in. "Like? Or more?"

"More?"

Riley stood up, ran over, and hugged her friend. "I'm so proud of you, Teagan. You're finally opening up and letting someone in."

Teagan beamed at that. "I am and it feels pretty damn amazing."

Flapping a French fry in her hand, Riley said, "If you marry Gian, will that make us related?"

Teagan wrinkled her nose. "Gian is Dominic's brother through their mother. You're related to Dominic through your father. The Romanos are actually Gian's cousins, but he's adopted so legally they are also his brothers."

I groaned. "My brain is melting."

"Let's just say yes," Riley said with a smile.

"Yes," Teagan said with enthusiasm, "but we're not getting married. We just started dating."

"Sure you're not," Riley said cheerfully. "Oh my God, now I need to find someone. I thought I had more time. Do not have children without me."

Did Riley really think it was that easy? Wasn't it that kind of thinking that had led our mother to trust the man who had hurt her? Hadn't I just seen the same pattern playing out with Jade?

I could have gone off on a reality check rant, but Riley and Teagan both looked so damn happy. I didn't want to take that from them. People needed to make their own mistakes. God only knows, I'd made enough of my own. If they needed me, I'd be there to pick up the pieces just as I knew they'd do for me.

"I'm pretty sure you have time," Teagan assured her. "Although I intend to have five. So, you'll have to keep up."

Holy crap. That's a lot of kids. "The two of you are nuts," I said, but softened my criticism with a smile.

They exchanged a look and, in unison, said, "We know." Then laughed.

I didn't stay long after that. Distance was what I needed to sort through what still felt too crazy to be true.

The people my mother had always feared now had names and faces—the Corisis. Rather than returning to my mother's apartment, I headed off to a café where I spent a few hours reading everything I could about the family.

Not much of it was good.

My biological father had been known for being ruthless and above the law. Dominic had followed in his footsteps. Insanely rich, internationally powerful beyond what any family should be, and tainted by scandals . . . the Corisis were dangerous. If they were anything like my bio-father, my mother had been right to fear them.

I wouldn't begin to know how to fight them if they came for us. All I could do was hope they wouldn't and that my sister was smart enough to stay away from them. I texted her: **Mom won't handle this well.**

I know.

We should tell her together.

Okay. After a pause, Riley added: **We have two brothers and a sister, Kal. That's kind of exciting.**

I didn't need time to think about my response to that. **You and Mom are the only family I care about. Don't rush off and do something that will only hurt Mom more. She needs us on her side.**

I would never hurt Mom.

I didn't answer that text because Riley would never intentionally hurt anyone, but she did sometimes rush forward without thinking about the damage she might leave in her wake. In some ways, she was a boat dropping anchor without thought of what lay below.

When it only affected me, I did my best to accept that side of her, but I couldn't this time. Our mother had endured too much already. Riley needed to respect that.

The Corisis needed to as well.

I'd make sure of that—somehow.

Together, that night, we told our mother about our conversation with Teagan. Riley asked so many questions about our bio-father and his family that our mother excused herself to cry in the other room.

The next day things went just as badly. Mom begged Riley to have nothing to do with the Corisis, and although Riley promised not to, we all knew she couldn't keep that promise. Fucking Riley. She wanted everyone to be happy, and even though I was furious with her, part of me envied the way she saw the world.

To her, there was nothing broken that couldn't be fixed.

I'd stopped believing that was true a long time ago.

When the dust settled, I flew off to Europe to start my first international tour. I called home every day, talked about anything but the Corisis, worked out until I barely fit in a wetsuit, and told myself everything would be okay. It had to be.

I took Jade's book with me and jotted notes throughout it as I dove in areas that were mentioned in the book. If I found myself in an area near any of the marine biologists from the book, I sought ways to connect with them.

I didn't tell them I was a dancer, and they didn't ask. I told them I was a huge fan of their work, had them autograph the book, and was even invited on dives with a few of them. When my notes became too much for the margins of the book, I began to record them in a journal I kept on a laptop.

My entries all started the same way: **I wish you were here, Jade. Today I . . .**

Invio paid the bills and stayed on stage.

The real me hunkered down and made the best of the situation.

Even though I had no intention of sharing my journal with Jade, the idea of her kept me from losing my mind every time Dominic Corisi sent me a text or a voicemail saying he wanted to meet me.

I didn't want to meet him.

I was afraid I might kill him if I did.

CHAPTER FIVE

Jade

A FTER MONTHS OF not seeing Sasha and Nikki in person a trip home was a much-needed treat. We met at our regular table in our favorite breakfast restaurant. After putting in our food orders we sat back and simply smiled at each other.

Sasha rested a hand on her rounded stomach. "It's so good to see you."

"We chat online all the time. You see my face more than some of my coworkers do," I answered easily. I loved these ladies and there was no way distance would diminish our friendship.

Nikki looked me over before saying, "You look happy—and tan."

I brought a hand to my face. No amount of sunblock could counter the effects of being out in the sun all day almost every day. "I am. Right now, I'm with a state conservation agency and I'm low man on the team so I get assigned whatever everyone else doesn't want to do, but I don't mind. I'm learning about invasive species inland and aquatic plant permits. There is so much opportunity to move within departments once I prove myself."

"That's fantastic," Sasha said. "I was half-hoping you wouldn't like Florida, but I'm so glad to see you finally doing something you enjoy."

I let out a happy smile. "Every day is different, but I'm surrounded by people who get excited about the same things I do. On my day off a bunch of us volunteered for a sea turtle conservancy. We spent the day setting up artificial lighting that would lead them toward the ocean instead of across the street to well-lit hotels and condominiums. The beach nests are protected, but hatchlings instinctively crawl toward the brightest light, which used to be the waves. We can't stop people from encroaching on their territory, but we can give them a fighting chance to survive despite the change in their environment." When I finished, I made an apologetic face. "Sorry. You know how I get."

Nikki leaned in. "I miss having you drop in and pester me while I'm trying to study, but I'm so glad you didn't marry Robert."

Sasha kicked her under the table. "Don't bring him up."

I shrugged. "It doesn't bother me. Things were dicey with me and my grandparents when I canceled the wedding at the last minute. I'm still paying them back for the money they'd put toward it, but I was over Robert as soon as I found out about Daphne."

"You don't miss him? Not even a little?" Sasha asked.

I shook my head. "Weird, huh?"

Nikki rolled her eyes. "Your quick rebound probably has nothing to do with you meeting your soul mate that night."

The waitress delivered our drinks and I mixed sugar and cream into my coffee before answering. "I don't even remember saying that to you, but I know he and I shared a connection. I wouldn't have broken free and gone to Florida if I hadn't met him."

After sipping on her water, Sasha said, "I wish you'd included me in on the call that night. All we have is Nikki's take on it and she's so analytical."

Nikki shrugged. "What do you think I left out? She was drunk. He was a good guy who took her home. They talked. They seemed to have a lot in common. He said he wanted to stay in touch but must not have meant it because he ghosted her after she sent him a gift."

Sasha waved for Nikki to stop. "Yeah, that's not the version anyone wants to hear. Jade met a man who put a halt to his dream of also being a marine biologist so he could help his family. He encouraged her to follow hers. That's not a 'good guy'—that's a *good man*—the kind you don't let get away. And have you seen him?" She pulled up a photo of Kal from his latest tour and flashed it at Sasha and me. "I'm just saying that when all of that comes in this package you check to see if he got your gift. For all we know, he didn't."

Heat flooded my cheeks and I looked away. "Do you really think a man like that is pining for me? For anyone?

There was even a woman throwing herself at him when he was walking me to my room."

"Oh, so you do remember that night," Sasha said.

I met her gaze. "Not all of it, but a lot of it. He was very kind to me when he had no reason to be." My hand went to my lips.

"Did he kiss you?" Nikki asked. "You didn't tell me that."

The memory of his lips moving gently over mine came back with a vividness that warmed my cheeks more. "It wasn't worth mentioning."

Nikki and Sasha exchanged a look. Sasha said, "The man said he wanted to hear from you." She waved her phone. "We all know where he is. All I'm suggesting is that you send him a DM."

Thankfully the food arrived and temporarily took the attention off me. I was chewing on a bite of egg when Nikki said, "I agree with Sasha."

I hurried to swallow before saying, "Hold on. You never agree with Sasha."

"That's not true," Nikki said with a smile. "We both think it's not healthy for you to turn away every man who asks you out while waiting for a text from a man who may never contact you."

"Every man?" I countered. "Three men have asked me out since I've been in Florida. Only three."

"That's two more than have asked me out," Nikki said.

"You don't even like men," I protested.

"Exactly, I have a reason to turn them down. You don't. Not unless you admit that you want to be with your dancer, and if that's the case you need to do something about it or that will likely not happen either."

"First, he's not a dancer. He is helping his family by dancing; that's not the same thing. Second, some people come into your life for a season, some for a reason. Maybe all he was meant to be was a catalyst for me to break free of my grandparents. I love them, but I needed this."

"Give me your phone," Sasha said.

"No." The problem with old friends is they knew you almost better than you knew yourself.

Nikki's eyebrows rose. "She's hiding something all right."

"I'm not."

"Prove it," they said in unison.

Cornered and guilty, I had no recourse but to confess. "Okay, so maybe I've been documenting my journey and saving photos Kal might want to see in a folder with his name on it."

"And?" Sasha pressed.

I groaned. "I may also have a spreadsheet of his tour schedule—but that's so I know he's okay. He hasn't canceled a show yet."

Nikki frowned. "Why are you so afraid to message him? What's the worst thing that could happen?"

I sat back and asked myself the same question. "I was drunk when we met. I have this beautiful memory of an incredible man who cared enough about me to make sure I made it home safely. What if he's nothing like how I remember him?"

Nikki nodded. "What if he's like Robert, is what you're worried about?"

I made a face. "I thought Robert was a good man. I mean, I almost married him."

Sasha placed her hand on my arm. "I get it. Sometimes my husband leaves the toilet seat up and when I forget to check at night, I've had some unpleasant bidet-like experiences."

Nikki turned to look at her. "I don't think that's what a bidet is like at all."

Sasha continued, "The point is, I can't live my life worried that every toilet will disappoint me."

"No, you could just teach your husband to put the seat down," Nikki said.

Sasha waved both hands near her head. "Jade knows what I'm saying."

I moved my head back and forth. "I think I do. I can't worry that every man will be like Robert." I winked at Nikki. "Or I really need to learn more about bidets."

Nikki laughed.

Sasha let out a dramatic sigh but smiled. "Wait until you're pregnant and discover the importance of a quickly available toilet and then you'll understand how spot-on the analogy was."

"No. No, I don't think we will." I met Nikki's gaze. We both shook our heads and laughed again.

"Whatever," Sasha gave her stomach another rub. "Don't listen to them. Nikki doesn't like to admit when I'm right and, this time, Jade is afraid to."

I took out my phone and spun it on the table beside my plate. "It's been months. What would I even say?"

Sasha's eyes were full of encouragement. "Less is more. Send him one of your photos with a quick note that you're thinking about him. Sometimes all a man needs to know is that you're still interested."

"That's it?" It sounded too easy.

Nikki pressed her lips together then said, "I hate to say it, but I agree with Sasha again. You may never know how he feels about you or if he even got your gift if you don't reach out to him. You may find out he is as wonderful as you remember, or you may learn that you built up a fantasy version of him that no man can live up to. Either way, I don't think it's healthy to compare every man to one you're not even sure exists."

"I don't—" I stopped myself there because it wasn't worth lying to them or myself. That was exactly what I'd been doing. Sure, Kal was gorgeous and deliciously built up. Divers in general, though, were pretty fit. My attraction to him had been on a much deeper level.

Beneath his anger and his stage persona, there was some-one who wanted more than the life he felt trapped in. From the little he'd told me about his family I understood he was bound by something stronger than what he had told me—his family needed him. My grandparents didn't rely on me financially. They'd sheltered me and worried for me, but all I'd risked when I walked away from that was their anger. And, honestly, they were already adjusting to the fact that I wanted to be more independent.

I didn't know what was at stake with his family, but I wanted to. Sasha and Nikki were right, I needed to send him a photo and a message. I considered all of his social media platforms, looked at a couple, found an email address for him and decided to use that. If he was anything like me, messages could sit for months on some of the platforms, but I checked my email daily.

On my phone, under the watchful eye of my two best friends I wrote: **This is me setting up lights on Juno Beach to help save hatchling sea turtles. Wish you were here.** I attached a photo from the day I'd volunteered for the conservancy. My hair was flying wild in the wind, I was carrying lighting equipment, and there were several others in the photo with me. We were all smiling.

I hit send before I had a chance to change my mind. "I did it."

Sasha gave my shoulder a pat. "If he's interested, you'll hear from him now."

I held the phone to my chest and let out a long breath. "If he's interested . . ." Even though I'd checked my text messages daily since I'd sent him the book, it probably would have been a bad idea to get involved with anyone back when my entire life had been in a tailspin. I was settled now and ready to see if what I thought I'd felt for him was real.

I reread the email I'd sent him. Would he answer it?

I'd survive if he didn't, but the not knowing—that was the hardest part.

CHAPTER SIX

Kal

I STOPPED AT the bar to down a shot before leaving the latest club I'd performed at. Nothing felt right lately, not my show, not my mood—nothing. The source of my frustration was easy enough to determine. My life, the one I'd worked so hard to hold together, was coming apart at the seams.

Riley was not only spending time with the Corisis on a regular basis, she was also letting them into our private business. My mother's medical bills were paid off in full supposedly by a government grant. Her next surgery was already scheduled and would be fully covered by her insurance. Sure.

I told myself I was happy for her and it didn't matter who had made her surgery possible. But none of it felt right. I was angry with myself for not being happier for my mother and angry with Riley for . . . hell, I was just angry.

The situation was out of control. Dominic Corisi was circling my family, throwing money around like we could be bought. He hadn't respected my demand that he stay away from my mother and Riley. My mother was scared he would turn on Riley the first time she denied him, just as Antonio had with her, and I had no reason to believe my mother was wrong.

Antonio had wooed my mother with money, charm, and promises. How was that any different than what his son was doing? To what end? Why put so much effort into siblings he must have known existed. I didn't believe for a second that someone like him didn't.

As I was debating if I should do one last shot before heading out, a tall red-haired woman slid into the seat beside me. The bar was emptying so her intention wasn't a mystery. Without even looking at her, I said, "Sorry, not interested."

"Yes, that's become clear and why I was sent."

That gained my attention. "Sent?" My temper began to rise. "Dominic is hiding behind women now?"

She made a face. "Your brother isn't the hiding type. He's trying to respect that you're not ready to meet him yet."

I straightened to my full height. "Oh, I'm ready to meet him, but I doubt he's ready to hear what I have to say."

She sighed. "I was told to offer you some amazing things, but I get the feeling you wouldn't accept anything from Dominic, would you?"

"How are you so observant and yet still here?"

Her chuckle was fuel on the flame of my irritation. "Sorry. It's just that I've known your brother for a long time, and you remind me so much of him. The glare you're giving me right now? Classic Dominic."

"I don't have time for this. Good night."

"Wait." Her tone softened. "Help me help both of you. I know what you don't want. Tell me what you *do* want."

I pinned her with a stare and growled, "I want to know that my family is safe. I don't want to go to jail for killing a brother I never knew I had because he can't resist finishing the work our father started. My mother has been through enough and my sister is too trusting to see how dangerous the Corisis are. Tell my brother what I want more than anything else is for my mother to stop crying because she's afraid of what he'll do to Riley. Tell him there is nothing he can say or do that will make me want anything to do with someone who let my mother suffer as long as he did. And what he's doing now? Too little too late—I don't trust his intentions. Tell him that."

The woman dabbed at the corner of one of her eyes. "I didn't know about your mother. If I had known, he would have. Your family was Antonio's best-kept secret." She sniffed. "I'm usually really good at uncovering things like this but there was no hint of your existence. Thomas knew but he kept his silence to protect you."

"I'm sorry, who the hell are you?"

"Alethea—"

"You know, I don't care."

She blocked my path when I moved to walk away. "You do. And Dominic does as well. Please hear me out. A lot has been going on while you've been away."

"That much I know."

"Give me five minutes. That's all I ask. If when I'm done you still don't want anything to do with the Corisis I'll go back and convince them to stay away from you and your family. But I don't think you'll want that. Five minutes and you won't have to deal with me chasing you down after all of your shows for the rest of your tour."

I folded my arms across my chest. "Five minutes. Starting now." I glanced at the clock on the register behind the bar.

"Dominic started off as a happy little boy, just like any other. Unfortunately, his father, your father, beat his mother on a regular basis. When he tried to protect her, he was beaten as well. Then one day his mother disappeared. Everyone thought she was dead, but she'd actually changed her name and gone into hiding in Italy. Dominic never stopped looking for her. It was only later, after Antonio's death, that his mother reappeared. To understand Dominic, you have to imagine what it was like for him to battle a man he couldn't win against, a man so cruel Dominic believed he'd murdered his mother and gotten away with it. Antonio was the devil incarnate. He destroyed more lives than anyone will probably ever know, but Dominic is nothing like him. He was one of his victims, no different than your mother. He might not have visible scars from him, but Dominic's just as damaged. Antonio's sins do not belong on his shoulders, but Dominic is driven to make amends for them anyway. I've never known anyone who has craved having a family more than Dominic does, without any idea of how to show people that he loves them. He'll manipulate situations, try to win your love by buying you things, and in general drive you crazy, but behind all of that is a man who is willing to learn to be whatever kind of brother you need him to be. All you have to do is believe in him enough to give him a chance and forgive him when he messes up because his intentions are always good." She took a breath at the end and waited.

It was a lot to process and as well as believe. "My mother wants nothing to do with him."

"She will. Riley is already winning her over. Your sister is relentless when it comes to bringing everyone together."

"You've met my sister?"

"And Gavin, the man I bet she marries. That man has balls. Not many people stand up to Dominic and he did that right out the gate. I approve of him. Dominic does too."

I wasn't proud to admit, "I don't know anything about Gavin. I haven't spoken to Riley much lately."

"I know. And I understand why. This isn't the kind of situation anyone could prepare for. I realize you have no reason to believe me, but I am rooting for all of you. Bend just a little and you just might find that none of this is as bad as it seems. You have a spitfire niece, Judy, and a too smart for his own good nephew, Leonardo, who have already added you to their nightly prayers. The only thing stopping you from being part of their lives is you."

I waved a hand at the club around me. "I'm sure I'd be a fabulous influence on them."

The redhead laughed. "Oh, honey, you'd have to try a hell of a lot harder to shock anyone I know." She sobered. "And you can leave this life behind you if you want. Nothing is holding you here."

"Except a solid contract."

"Already dealt with. You're free to go anytime you want to." She bit her bottom lip. "I did mention that Dominic has issues with boundaries, didn't I?"

I sat down, torn between wanting to dismiss everything she'd said and wanting to believe her. "How is Riley winning my mother over?"

"It's not just her." The woman took out her phone and showed me a photo of my mother smiling at an older gentleman in a way I'd never seen her look at anyone before "His name is Hamilton Wenham. He's Gavin's father and sweet on your mother. The two are adorable together."

What the hell? "She hasn't mentioned him."

"It's quite new, but he dotes on her."

"Why do you have a photo of them?"

She wrinkled her nose and shrugged. "I'm Dominic's eyes and ears. Needing to know more than I should has been a lifelong gift and curse. Dominic and my husband are really the only two who understand me. I guess that's why I'm so loyal to Dominic. He's never judged me."

"Dominic doesn't sound like someone who'd hurt my sister or my mother."

The woman's eyes misted. "He'd give his life for them— and for you. You're his family."

"His family," I repeated the words and looked away. I sighed, not sure how much of this I should believe. If what she'd said about Dominic was true, he was no more guilty for what had happened than my mother was. Riley was happy to have the Corisis in her life. My mother didn't appear to be crying anymore. Maybe it was time to meet this brother of mine—see for myself what kind of person he was. I went to say as much to the red-haired woman, but she was gone.

I took out my phone to send Dominic a text when I noticed that I had an email. Normally I would have waited until the next day to read it, especially since I had so much else on my mind, but something told me it was important.

It was from JTremblay. My heart started pounding wildly as I opened it and read: **This is me setting up lights on Juno Beach to help save hatchling sea turtles. Wish you were here.**

I read the message again then lost myself in the smiling eyes of the woman who had been on my mind every day since we'd met. *Jade.*

Wish you were here . . . She'd ended her message the same way I'd started every journal entry to her.

And I'm free to go to her . . .

CHAPTER SEVEN

Jade

I T WASN'T A wetsuit day or even a leave-the-office day. I'd spent the last six hours double-checking a coworker's plant identification findings and documenting any discrepancies I found. It wasn't fun or a job that made me particularly popular with the team, but that was why it had fallen in my lap. They'd all done the same, starting out, and made it through. I would as well.

As a child when I'd dreamed about being a marine biologist, I'd imagined someone holding a shark's mouth open while I counted its teeth and exciting things like that. In college I'd listened to the field stories of my professors and imagined myself flying off to exotic places as soon as I graduated.

The field was much more competitive than that. Those experiences were out there but to have them I'd have to get my masters and then likely a PhD as well. I was ready to take that next step or would be right after I finished paying my grandparents back. Canceled weddings are expensive, especially when the man you decided not to marry wants nothing to do with the bills. I probably could have gone after him legally, but that wasn't where I wanted to put my energy. Onward and upward.

I had just closed down my computer when a text came in from a number I didn't recognize. **Sitting on Juno Beach next to the pier. Wish you were here. Kal.**

A photo came in of him in a T-shirt with the ocean as a backdrop. My breath caught in my throat, and I nearly dropped my phone. *Holy shit. He's in Florida. How? Why? To see me? What should I write?* With shaking hands, I typed: **I can be there in about thirty-three minutes.**

I reread my text and groaned—*Way to sound desperate to see him.*

I also could have been less specific. I only knew how long it would take me to get there because I remembered the time it had taken from this office to that beach when I'd volunteered there.

Don't rush. Unless you want to.

I want to. **I just finished work for the day, so this is perfect timing.**

Hungry?

In more ways than I'm ready to admit. **Starving.**

There's a restaurant across the street. I can have something waiting here for you on the beach or I can wait, and we can eat inside.

The beach. I'm not a picky eater. Just no pickles, please. I don't like them.

Awesome. Text me when you get here.

I will.

I said a hasty goodbye to the two other people in the office and sprinted to my car only to realize that I'd left my purse with my key fob in my desk. As I made my way back into the office, I told myself to breathe and relax.

That didn't stop me from calling Sasha as soon as I was on the road. "He's here," I said in a rush. "Kal texted me and he's waiting for me at the Juno Beach pier. Right now. I'm on my way to see him."

"Slow down," Sasha said with a laugh. "So did he get your gift?"

"I don't know. I didn't ask. He must have gotten my email, though. I can't believe he's here." I checked my face in the rearview mirror. "Shit, I'm going to see him in jeans and a work shirt. I didn't even stop to put on makeup. What if I get there and he's gone?"

"Why would he be gone?"

I returned my attention to the road and gripped the steering wheel. "Because he doesn't feel real. I've thought about him so much. What if he's nothing like I remember? What if I'm not what he remembers?"

"You were drunk and crying when he met you. Let's hope you're different."

"Right. And whatever he saw in me will still be there."

"If he came to see you, he already likes you."

"According to his tour schedule he should be in Singapore. Why isn't he? He's missing a show and he never does that." A thought occurred to me. "What if something terrible happened? Oh, my God, maybe someone he knew died. I'm fantasizing about him naked, and he could be in town for a funeral."

"Jade, stop. He's probably here to see you."

"In the middle of his tour? Why would he do that?"

"I don't know, but that's something you could ask him when you see him."

I took a deep calming breath. "Sasha, he's here."

"I know, hon."

"What if he's only here because it's highly likely that I'll say yes to sex with him?"

"My guess is that if he's only looking for sex, he could have found some in Singapore."

"You're right. Still, I should take things slowly with him until I'm sure."

"Some of the best sex I've had with my husband was when we were first together and figuring things out. That's not to say sex isn't great now, but there's just an intensity to it in the beginning when emotions are running high."

"So I *should* sleep with him?"

Sasha chuckled. "Yes, that's what I'm saying. Not. You should let things unfold the way they're meant to. Go meet him. Be careful, but not so careful that you overthink things and cheat yourself of the wonder. This time don't be who you should be—just be yourself and let him be whoever he is. Maybe you'll click, maybe you won't. But at least it'll be real."

I took another deep breath. "You're brilliant, you know that? You could do this for a living."

"If I wanted to but I don't. The closer I get to my baby arriving, the less everything else matters. I don't want someone else to raise her. I want to be a stay-at-home mom. Before you say anything, that is not a cop-out. Keeping a house and raising children is just as important as having a career."

Her tone pulled me away from my own excitement to be there for her. "Sasha, you don't have to convince me. I wish my mother had made better choices and been there to raise me. But even if she hadn't died, she wouldn't have put me first. That wasn't her. Your baby is one lucky kid."

Sasha sniffed. "Sorry, I'm feeling emotional today. I needed to hear that." She let out an audible breath. "Now, back to Kal. I'm going to be sitting by the phone waiting for you to tell me all about how this date goes."

"He offered to get some food from a restaurant so we can eat on the beach when I get there."

"So, he's considerate."

"I told him no pickles."

"You and your damn pickle aversion. Did you have a traumatic pickle incident as a child?"

"I just don't like how they taste. I don't think it's deeper than that. I'm not a vinegar person."

"I bet your grandparents put pickles on everything and told you to like it."

Weird, they had, but I hadn't made that connection. "How do you always know these things?"

"Because I know you. People are not all that complicated. We all want to be loved. We all resent when we feel that we have no control over our lives. You love your grandparents and for a long time you did everything you could to make them happy, but that wasn't easy. The pickles were your rebellion."

"Wow, when it comes to rebelling, I sure chose a pathetic hill to die on."

"Or a safe one, one that you knew wouldn't hurt anyone. You've got a big heart, Jade. And you're a pleaser, which isn't necessarily a bad thing. But you're happy in Florida because you're finally standing up for yourself and creating healthy boundaries. My only caution with Kal is that, from what you've said about him, he is struggling to find those for himself. You may need to be patient while he figures his out."

Sasha's words touched my heart. I didn't know Kal, but I wanted to and that wouldn't happen from one shared meal on a beach. What I needed to do was stop overthinking it and, as she'd said, let it unfold as it was meant to.

To lighten the mood, I asked, "So I *shouldn't* sleep with him?"

"Lord, give me patience."

I laughed. "I'm almost there, Sasha. Thank you for talking me through this. I feel a lot better now."

"Good. I'll tell Nikki what's going on. We'll both want details tonight . . . or tomorrow. Whenever."

"Will do. Thanks again." I ended the call as I pulled into the beach's parking lot.

Kal rose to his feet and shaded his eyes with one hand when I stepped out of my car. I started walking toward him. He started walking toward me.

We met in the middle and as if it were the most natural thing in the world, he cupped my face and we kissed hungrily. There were no questions, no worries as time suspended and we gave ourselves over to a desire so primal it pushed all thoughts from my head.

His lips were demanding and skilled. His tongue teased my lips to open for him. My ability to deny him anything in that moment was zero. I surged against him, rose onto my tiptoes and craved more than was possible with our clothing on.

When he raised his head, I felt shattered and healed all at once. His breathing was as ragged as mine. The crooked smile he beamed down at me melted my heart. "Sorry. I guess I'm excited to see you."

Evidence of how excited was straining the front of his swim trunks. My voice was breathless as I said, "I'm not complaining."

He rested his forehead on mine. "Thank you for meeting me here."

"You're welcome," I said in a strangled voice.

He tilted his head back a little so he could look into my eyes. "I loved the book you sent me."

"You did get it."

"I did." He pressed his lips together then said, "I should have sent you a message then, but——"

"But?" Had he been in a relationship? Just not been interested? Did I want to know?

He searched my face for a moment. "I wasn't in a good headspace." He stepped back, breaking contact. "I'm still not."

"I don't know what that means."

He touched the side of my face with a hand. "Are you happy in Florida?"

All I could be was honest. "Very."

He smiled. "That matters to me more than anything else. I want to hear about your job and your life here."

I nodded. We should talk. I glanced past him and laughed. "Did you leave our food on your towel?"

"I did." He spun in time to witness several seagulls feasting on our dinner. "Shit. Sorry."

Kal was even more built than I remembered. His sheer size would intimidate most people, but when he looked down at me there was none of the anger I remembered from his stage act. His boyishly guilty smile was endearing, and I laughed. "How about I buy the next round and we guard it with our lives?"

He seemed about to protest, but then nodded. "You're

on."

We headed to the beach to collect his things then to a restaurant down the street that had outdoor tables overlooking the water.

CHAPTER EIGHT

Kal

S ITTING ACROSS FROM Jade, with the backdrop of ocean waves behind her, I took a breath and savored the perfection of the moment. Each time I asked her a question about her job or her move she seemed surprised I was not only listening but interested.

Had no one celebrated her accomplishments? Was she unaware that the beauty of who she was on the inside brought a glow to her physical looks and made her irresistible? Smart, funny, caring . . . I would have been attracted no matter what she looked like, but she had that as well.

No, she wasn't the type to turn every man's head. The eyes of some men were drawn by flash and fake. Big hair, big tits, flawless skin. That wasn't Jade. I loved her lean body, that she didn't have a stitch of makeup on, that I wanted to kiss the freckles on the bridge of her nose, and that I'd be able to smell the ocean in her windblown hair when we fucked.

Not that we would on that visit. That wasn't why I was there. This—seeing her, confirming that she'd made the leap to somewhere better—that's what my soul had needed.

She ducked her head then smiled up at me shyly. "Sorry, I don't normally talk about myself so much. You must be bored."

That was enough for me to reach for her hand. "Do I look bored?"

I let my need for her show in my eyes. The air between us sizzled and her hand gripped mine tighter. "No," she whispered.

I bent so our faces were closer. "Are you?"

She swallowed visibly. "No."

I raised a hand and ran a thumb lightly across her bottom lip. "I like the way you say no, but I bet I'm going to love when you say yes."

Her face flushed and her breath warmed my thumb. "Is that your go-to line with women?"

It was a valid question. As I played my words back in my head, they did sound like something a man would say when he was on the hunt. I moved my hand to caress her jaw and the smooth-as-silk skin behind her ear. "I don't need lines."

Her eyebrows shot up and she barked out a laugh. "Wow, your ego is . . . impressive."

I chuckled. "That came out wrong."

There was humor in her eyes as she asked, "What would have been the right way?"

I withdrew my hand. "And here I was thinking that you're a nice person."

She didn't back down. "Oh, I'm nice, but I'm also curious. What's it like to be you?"

I opened my mouth to say something playful, but held it back and asked, "How real do you want me to get?" I regretted my question as soon as I'd voiced it because the tone of our conversation as well as the expression in her eyes instantly changed.

She said, "As real as you're comfortable being with me."

I shifted back in my seat and ran both hands over my face before leaning forward again and looking her right in the eye. "I don't know anymore. Things used to make sense, even what I was angry about did. My entire life is upside down right now and I'm just trying to find my footing."

"Do you want to talk about it?" She voiced the question with such sincerity I was humbled by it. She deserved so much better than I was bringing to her.

"Not yet." No, I refused to lay the whole abusive father, rich dangerous brother, impulsive sister shit at her door. "I should have stayed away until my head was straight, but I wanted to see you."

She searched my face. "Are you married?"

My lips twisted in a smile. "I wish it were that simple."

"I don't." She let out a sigh. "Running from a loan shark?"

"No. Are those even a real thing?"

"I have no idea." She shrugged then leaned closer. "Give me something. Is it the reason you're here rather than on tour?"

She was good. "It is, actually."

"Okay."

Days had gone by since I'd decided to call Dominic and I had yet to do so. I'd flown to Florida to see Jade without even calling home to tell my family I'd canceled the rest of my tour. Frustrated with myself, I growled, "I can't tell if things are getting better or worse. I don't know how to protect the people I love or if I'm even supposed to. I have so much anger inside of me and I don't know what to do with it or who I am without it." My hands fisted on the table, and I saw her eyes widen with concern. I relaxed my hands. "That didn't come out right, either." I groaned. "I should go."

She stopped me from leaving by lightly touching my arm. "Why are you here, Kal?"

I tried to find the words to articulate it but couldn't. Instead, I reached down to the bag I'd brought with me to the beach, pulled out the book she'd sent me and pushed it across the table to her. It looked ragged, a little water damaged, and I had no idea what her reaction to what I'd done with it would be. "Open it."

She did. As she read one of her hands came up to her mouth. She began to flip through the book, scouring my notes without saying anything then looked up at me. "You did all this since we met?"

"And more. I started a journal as well."

With one hand flat on a page of the book, she said, "You sought out everyone in the book and met them?"

"Not all of them, but most."

"And you dived with them? Kal, this is incredible."

"The book inspired me to reach out to them—you inspired me. I wrote everything down so I'd remember what to thank you for."

She glanced over my notes in the book and read one aloud. "I wish you were here, Jade. Today I . . ." then asked, "These notes are all for me?"

To lighten the mood a little, I joked, "I guess that depends on if you think they're romantic or too much."

When she met my gaze again, her eyes were brimming with tears. "They're beautiful and I don't really care how messed up you are, I'm glad you're here."

I laughed. "That's—"

Her face went red. "I didn't mean . . ."

I kissed her then. It felt better than anything either of us could have said. She met my passion with her own and for a moment nothing else mattered. Only location and what was left of our restraint kept the kiss from progressing. I broke it off and we sat there simply staring into each other's eyes without speaking.

Eventually she whispered, "Can I show you something?"

"Sure," I answered in an equally hushed voice.

She dug her phone out of her purse and brought up a photo on it. "That's me in Michigan packing for Florida. I took that picture for you."

I moved my chair closer, put an arm around the back of hers, and breathed her in while looking at the screen. "Tell me you're not a Tigers fan."

She nodded shamelessly.

"That's a problem. I'm a Red Sox fan."

She chuckled breathlessly. "Glad we sorted that out before we got attached to each other."

"I might be able to get over it." I bent and nuzzled her neck. "I'm already attached."

She shuddered against me. "Me too." The cheeky look she gave me had my heart thudding. "But sorry, I can't be with a Red Sox fan."

My answer was to kiss my way up her neck to her ear. "I bet I could change your mind."

Her quickened breathing matched exactly how I was feeling. I didn't want to be in public with her anymore. All the reasons why I felt we should take things slowly fell right out of my head. She cleared her throat and asked, "Would you like to go somewhere quieter where I could show you . . . more photos?"

I kissed her again then growled, "I'm up for whatever you want."

She paid the bill and I let her because my mind was racing with all the ways I would repay her that night. I also agreed that she should drive for the same reason.

CHAPTER NINE

Jade

I DIDN'T ASK myself if we were going too fast, because how I felt around Kal didn't leave room for such questions. Every inch of my body was focused on him and impatiently craving his touch. His must have felt the same because I'd barely pulled out of the parking lot before he released his seat belt and shifted so he could reach me better.

He kissed my neck and shoulder while yanking the front of my shirt free of my jeans. His touch was forceful and exciting. This was a man who knew what he wanted and what he wanted was me. His hand was strong and rough, but oh so skilled as it slid up my stomach and beneath my bra, pushing it above my breasts so they were freed for him to explore.

I fought to keep my eyes glued to the road as he took one of my nipples between his thumb and finger and rolled it in the most delicious way then moved to the other to do the same. All the while, he kissed my neck, the shell of my ear, and told me how much he wanted me.

When his hand moved to the snap of my jeans, I shifted

my hips to allow him access. He didn't need more than that to drag down the zipper and plunge his hand down the front of my underclothing. His touch was just as skilled there. Not rushed. Not tentative. He worked magic on and around my clit until I was writhing against his hand and begging for more. When he dipped a thick finger inside me, I spread my legs wider.

His finger filled me and worked a spot others had found elusive. I pulled the car over onto a darkened road and turned the engine off. It was all on then.

I undid my seat belt and shifted so my back was on the driver's door. Between kisses, he yanked my shoes off then we worked together to hastily remove my jeans. Bared before him, he thrust two fingers inside me and began to pump in and out while also pulling my shirt upward and taking one of my small breasts into his mouth.

His teeth teased my nipple. His tongue circled and worshipped. The heat from his breath tickled and brought more pleasure. All the while his hand fucked me, taking me from begging to nearly sobbing with need. I wrapped my arms around his neck, and I cried out his name as I came and shuddered around his hand as it gentled inside me.

He withdrew his hand and moved to kiss his way across both of my bared breasts again then down my stomach. His unrushed speed was a sweet torture. I was small, he was strong, the space was tight, but he lifted my legs and positioned his head between them.

When his mouth claimed my core, I couldn't help but grasp the steering wheel and the back of my seat. His tongue circled and flicked. It plunged and withdrew. Each time I felt he couldn't excite me more, he found a way to.

When I thought he might send me over the edge for a second time, he raised his head and said, "I have a condom in my back pocket."

I ran my hand down his back, over his tight still-clothed ass and took my time locating that foil package. I eagerly adjusted our position so I could lower the front of his swim trunks and free his hard cock. I sheathed him and climbed onto his lap.

His kiss mirrored the wild hunger raging within me. He pulled his shirt off over his head. I shed my shirt and bra so we could be as skin-to-skin as the situation allowed.

Hands on my hips, he moved his tip back and forth over my sex while our tongues circled each other, and I whimpered with excitement. I gasped as he thrust upward into me, then deepened our connection with a thrust of my own.

We fit so perfectly I could have wept from the pleasure of it. Our rhythm was slow and sure at first then became less controlled and wilder. Up and down, deeper and harder. It was gloriously freeing and so much better than I'd ever experienced that I didn't want it to end.

Nothing that intense could last forever. He came just before I did but kept pumping into me as I joined him. As I came back to earth, I slumped against him. He wrapped his arms around me, my head tucked beneath his chin, his heart beat loudly in my ear.

Neither of us spoke. I wondered if it was always like that for him because what we'd shared had changed my thoughts on sex. Once a week would never be enough.

He kissed the top of my head. "So much for taking things slowly with you."

I tipped my head back so I could meet his gaze. There was a sadness in his eyes I hadn't expected to see, and it tugged at my heart. In an attempt to make him smile I repeated his earlier question, "Do I look bored?"

He smiled, but not all the way to his eyes. "You matter to me, Jade."

I brought a hand to the stubble on his chin. "This would be an awkward time to tell me if I didn't."

That did have his eyes shining with humor. "That it would be." He took a deep breath. "I have a hotel room near the beach."

"I have an apartment about fifteen minutes away."

He chuckled. "You know what I'm asking."

"Do I?" I asked, even though I did.

He kissed me again in the most gloriously mind-erasing way, then murmured against my lips, "Do you want to continue this somewhere more private?"

"Duh."

His expression was priceless.

I joked, "Yeah, I *duhed* you. Is there anything about

what's going on here that suggests I don't want it to continue?"

He shook his head. "No. I just didn't expect you to be so . . . open about it."

That made me do a quick self-assessment. "Normally I'm not, but a friend of mine told me to relax—just be me and let you be you."

"I like your friends already." He ran a hand through my hair then eased me off his lap. "My place or yours—you choose."

I shimmied my shirt back over my head, tossed my bra in the backseat, then pulled on my jeans again while I considered both options. His was closer. How far did I want to let him into my life? When I glanced his way, he was covered again and relaxed.

I needed the truth, regardless of what it was. "My answer depends on if this visit is all we'll have or the start of something." I closed my eyes briefly and looked out the front of the car rather than into his eyes. "I'm okay either way, but if you're going to fly off tomorrow, I need to know."

"I can't stay past a day or two." His words cut through me. "I want to hide out here with you, but there are things I have to go back and face."

I nodded without looking at him. "Okay."

He laid a hand on my thigh. "Don't say it's okay when that's not how you feel."

I let out an angry breath and turned to him. "What do

you want, Kal? If you're looking for someone who'll beg you to stay, that's not me. I'm finally in a good place and I'm building a life I like. If you want to be with me, be with me. If you don't, that's fine. I'll keep living my life and you keep doing you. I'm not looking for games, though."

"I'm not either." He ran a hand through his hair. "I've thought about you every day since we met."

I turned in my seat to face him. "I thought about you too. All the time. So much more than I should have so soon after breaking off an engagement." As my words hung in the silence, I wondered if I wasn't being *too* me. Was this level of honesty a relationship builder or killer? I'd certainly never spoken this way to Robert. I'd held back with him. I didn't want to do that with Kal.

"Want to take a walk on the beach?" he asked.

The sun was going down, and the calming sound of the waves always brought me peace. "I'd love that."

We drove to a closer beach than the one I'd met him at, parked, and he grabbed his towel from his bag before we headed down a wooden boardwalk to the sand. He laid the towel parallel to the water and we sat side by side.

With his arms resting on his drawn-up knees, he looked out over the waves. "I've made a lot of mistakes in my life, but I've never not known how to make things right before."

I was falling hard and fast for a man I didn't know how to comfort. "When I feel that way, I call my friends."

He shook his head. "I don't have many of those anymore. When I started dancing, I left my old friends behind. I now have circles of people eager to party with me, but none I can be real with."

I almost reached for him but kept my hands on the towel beside me. "You can be real with me." When his eyes sought mine there was such torment in them that I scooted closer to him and wrapped my arms around him. His earlier words came back to me, and I modified them to what I hoped he needed to hear. "You'll feel a lot better when you free yourself from the belief that you're supposed to have all the answers. No one does. We're all just doing our best to figure this whole life thing out."

He put his arm around me and kissed my temple. "You're a good person, Jade."

"And you're not?"

He sighed. "I've tried to be. What would you say if I told you rather than being grateful to the person who paid off my mother's medical bills, I'm angry with him? And worse? That same person paid off the tour company, allowing me to get out my contract and cancel the tour. I could have refused the gift, but apparently I wanted to be free more than I wanted to respect myself."

"We all want to be free, Kal. I understand that more now than I ever did before." My heart broke for him even as I tried not to guess wildly at what sort of person would throw money around like that and what their motivation could be.

"I sold my soul to the devil. Literally. There's a town in

Italy that actually calls him that. I wasn't surprised when I read that in an article."

"*Who* is this man?"

"My half brother. Our father was the man who shattered the vertebrae in my mother's back. He's the reason she's suffered for so long."

"Your brother?"

"No, our bio-father."

"Which one does the Italian town call the devil?"

"My brother. It was an old article. I don't know what they call him now. For all I know it might be something worse."

I took a moment to digest what he was saying. "So, out of the blue your brother paid off your mother's medical bills and your contract?"

"It's more complicated than that."

I cuddled closer to his side. "I'm right here. Tell me."

He met my gaze. "I grew up in Lockton, Mass, with my mother and sister. We never had much, but the only hard part was watching my mother struggle with pain. I don't have much money saved because I poured everything I made into her bills." He took a breath. "That's not a complaint, just a reality."

"And a loving thing to do."

He took another deep breath. "If I'm so loving, why can't I be happy that my mother can finally have that surgery we've been working toward? We didn't know about my brother until recently and when we found out about him, my mother was terrified he'd make our family suffer the way our father did."

"And you wanted to protect her."

"I did, but I couldn't. Riley, that's my twin sister, has such a big heart. As soon as she heard we had family we didn't know, she couldn't stay away from them. Now she's dating some rich guy and my mother is with his father. Don't ask. I still can't picture it. My mother. I've never seen her show any interest in dating. Everything is changing so fast, and I don't know if I should nod and go along with it or fight to save them." His expression tightened. "As if I could win that fight. How do you fight someone with so much money that even I couldn't resist the lure of saying yes to him?"

None of this was what I expected him to say he was dealing with, but I didn't doubt the truth of it. "What is your brother like?"

"I don't know. I haven't spoken to him directly yet." He brought a hand up to rub his forehead. "I told myself it was time to, but I came here instead."

Tears welled in my eyes. "Because you needed a friend."

He sniffed and looked away. "Not quite living up to the Invio vibe, am I?"

I hugged him tighter. "I wouldn't take Invio home with me, but Kal is welcome anytime."

He pulled me onto his lap and encircled me with those

muscular arms of his, but I understood it was my strength he needed—just as I'd needed his that night in Vegas. "I have to go back and face this. And I need to do it in a way that keeps my family safe while allowing them to make their own happiness. I don't know what that looks like." After burying his face in my hair, he said, "I told you I was fucked up."

That wasn't how I saw him at all. I laid my head on his chest and said, "Life is easy for assholes. They don't give a shit about anyone else. Being a good person is hard. You're not fucked up, the situation you're in is. I don't know what I'd do in your place."

He looked into my eyes. "Thank you for letting me talk this out."

I traced his strong jaw. "Thank you for making sure I made it home safely in Vegas. I needed a friend that night and you were one. Your encouragement was what I needed to believe in myself and break free. Regardless of how you got here, you're free now too. And I believe in you. You're going to figure this out, and when you do . . . you'll understand why I'm so grateful to you."

A spark of something lit in his eyes and he asked, "For more than the orgasms?"

I shrugged. "Oh, those . . . I can do that for myself."

His eyebrows rose then he started to laugh, and I joined in. When we settled again, he said, "I have an idea, what do you think of going back to your place and having sex until we both forget how you almost had me bawling on this beach, because neither Invio nor Kal are into that."

I chuckled. "How much sex would that require?"

He helped me to my feet and tossed the towel over his shoulder. "Hours probably."

"Hours," I repeated as my body began to hum for his again. "I have a really good memory. It might take days."

"I can do that too." He spun me into his arms and kissed me soundly. I didn't tell him that that was enough to wipe everything else from my mind. I'd never felt as connected to a man or as uninhibited. I knew he needed to leave, but I wasn't about to say or do anything to rush that along. Thank God for weekends.

CHAPTER TEN

Kal

THE NEXT MORNING, sated from several sessions of lovemaking, I didn't want to leave Jade's bed. Partly due to how good her naked body felt curled against mine, but there was so much more. I liked being with her—really liked it.

She was flipping through photos she'd taken since moving to Florida, telling me the details behind each. I loved there were so many where she wasn't alone. She went to the beach and went diving with people from work. She'd volunteered with groups all over Florida and there were photos of her out on their boats or at their work sites.

She was in a good place, building the life she wanted, just as she'd said. Knowing that she was okay felt almost as good as sex with her had. Should I have stayed away until I got my head straight?

As if she could sense the change in my mood, she turned in my arms so she could see my face. "What are you thinking?"

I'd gotten used to people not caring to know more than

my surface. Jade needed more from me and the last thing I wanted to do was disappoint her, so I was honest. "I was thinking about how amazing you are for taking a hit and not letting it keep you down. You stood up, dusted yourself off, and look at you now."

Her smile warmed my heart. "I am pretty happy with myself. Sometimes I wish I'd done this earlier, but maybe I had to go through some crap to appreciate where I am now."

I was several steps behind her on that journey. "I'm determined to get to that place, but I'm not there yet. I'm thinking I should come back when I have my shit together."

"This is about more than your brother." There was no judgment in her eyes. "What do you think you need to do to be where I am?"

Her question echoed in me. I was quiet until the answer began to come to me. "I don't have a college degree, a job, or even a car. If we're speaking honestly, 'former stripper' doesn't open a lot of doors. I'm starting over with nothing."

She tucked a hand under her head and simply held my gaze. "You need a plan."

I nodded. "I could make fast money if I returned to the stage, but I don't want that. I could bartend but I'm trying to get out of the bar scene. Over the years I've been approached for modeling. I'd hate it, but I could do it. I'm not afraid of hard work. The goal is to return to college, but I won't qualify for financial aid due to my recent high income. I could take out loans, but to do that I need a job. It's all doable, but I'm going to be cash strapped for a few years."

She searched my face. "So many people would take the easy money."

"I've gone down that road, and I almost lost myself."

Shifting closer to me, she caressed the side of my face. "How long after you graduate will you need to work before you think we should be together? Do you have a set amount you'll need in the bank? I have high standards, you know."

She was giving me shit. "I'm being serious."

The understanding in her eyes melted my concerns away. "Most of my spare money is going to pay my grandparents back for the wedding that didn't happen. I don't have a nest egg, a trust fund, or even a car that's paid off, but I don't care. As soon as I do have some cash, I'll be heading back to school for my masters."

"So, what you're saying is that we could be poor together." A smile spread across my face, and I stopped her before she answered seriously. "For *years*."

"Yep, that's what I'm saying." Her smile warmed me to my toes.

It sounded heavenly. "We could have naked study sessions."

She laughed. "We'd get nothing done."

I wrapped my arms around her and cuddled her closer. "It would take practice, lots and lots of practice, but we should have goals." The kiss we shared was passionate but bubbling with friendship and laughter. I ended it by rolling onto my back and hauling her partially on top of me. "What do you want to do today?"

"I was invited to join a group of interns as they place some BRUVs—those are baited remote underwater videos. It's not glamourous. We go out on a small boat, bait and drop the cameras, then hang out for a few hours. After we pull up the cameras, we upload the video; analyze the footage; record diversity, abundance, and any unusual behavior; then input it into the state database. This is part of a long-term study. We're not expecting to see anything out of the ordinary today. Technically the interns are qualified to do it without me, and AI does most of the work in identifying the species, it's my job to review their work. I could do it on Monday, but I jump at any excuse to spend the day out on the water."

"Me too." I didn't want her to miss out, but I also didn't want her to feel she couldn't enjoy that without me. "Although, to be clear, I have no problem finding something to entertain myself with if you want to go and meet up later."

She gave me a tight hug. "Come, it'll be fun."

"How much time do we have before we meet them?"

After checking the clock beside her bed, she said, "Two hours or so."

"Good." I kissed her again, this time slowly and with more heat. I liked the idea of seeing her with her coworkers. I also liked the idea of a little more time alone with her.

She made a pleased sound deep in her throat and slid a hand down to encircle my cock. I knew I'd have to leave her the next day, but I pushed that thought far, far away and let myself enjoy being with her.

CHAPTER ELEVEN

Jade

RATHER THAN CALLING Sasha and Nikki, I sent them a text explaining that things were going really well with Kal, so well that I couldn't call them yet. They seemed to understand.

After a quick shared shower, I put a bathing suit on under a pair of shorts and a top. Kal wore the same swim trunks and shirt from the day before and we stopped at his hotel room to pick up more of his things.

When we met the interns at the dock, I was taken aback by their nervous vibe. Pete, Joe, and Lynn were normally super laid-back. We'd done the same outing a few weeks earlier with no hitch. Had something happened since?

It was when I introduced them that I realized the interns were reacting to Kal. Although he'd greeted each with an approachable smile, he towered over the two male interns. I could have sworn one of them tried to flex his bicep when he shook Kal's hand. My impression of Lynn had been that she was more interested in cataloging fish types than men until she saw Kal. Her instant adoration was almost comical.

Almost, if I hadn't been slightly tempted to hip check her into the water.

We settled onto the benches on either side of a boat that looked smaller than ever with Kal on it. Although I'd spent the last nearly twenty-four hours exploring and appreciating every muscular inch of him, it took seeing him next to the male interns for me to realize how normal men compared to him. There was no comparison. His chiseled features were classically good-looking. His body was muscled to just shy of being too much. Had Kal wanted to be in the movies he could have stolen parts from the most buff men in the business.

Unlike the last time we'd done this trip, there was very little conversation on the way to the first drop site. I wondered if Kal realized he was the reason.

When the boat slowed in preparation of dropping the first camera, I asked Kal if he'd like to learn how to bait it.

"Sure," he said. "What are you using?"

"Squid." I led him to the cooler where we had the meat and showed him how it needed to be folded over a few times to fit into the tube.

He watched closely but didn't look surprised by any of it. It was then I remembered a dive he'd noted in the book I'd sent him. "Did you do this when you dove with Bilboa?"

"Not the day we dove, but he let me join his team in Indonesia. They're studying the Raja Ampat."

That caught Pete's attention. He joined us and asked,

"You dove with Bilboa? Julian Bilboa? How? When?"

Kal looked from Pete to me as if requesting permission. I nodded once even though I wasn't sure how much he'd share or if it was wise to. Kal said, "Jade and I have been friends for a while. She sent me *Save the Ocean, Save the World: Stories from the World's Leading Marine Scientists*. Reading it inspired me to seek some of them out. I was doing a lot of traveling at the time, so whenever I found myself near someone mentioned in the book, I reached out to them. We'd talk and many of them offered to show me what they were working on."

Joe left Lynn at the wheel of the boat to come stand on the other side of Kal. "Just like that?"

With a humble expression, Kal shrugged. "I made sure I'd read the research of each biologist before I contacted them. It was intense. You don't get to where they are without publishing a substantial library of work, but that's the kind of reading I enjoy. So, when I met them, I not only knew what they were working on but what had led them there. That made connecting with them much easier since most people's favorite topic is themselves."

I packed the bait into the first BRUV, checked with Lynn that she was ready, then dropped it along with a buoy over the side of the boat. As soon as we stopped at the next site, she switched off with Joe and asked Kal, "Who else did you contact? Oh, my God, this is my dream. Tell us everything. What were they like? What did they show you?"

Kal packed the next few BRUVs while sharing stories of meeting the biggest names in marine science. He described their work with such a wealth of background knowledge and detail that we were all spellbound. None of what he shared came across as bragging. It might well have been a documentary, if they were delivered by a gorgeous man with a quiet sense of humor. Intelligent, well-spoken, an impassioned advocate for environmental issues—being Invio really must have been killing this man.

It was fascinating to watch Kal take the interns from being intimidated and attracted to him to wanting to join him on whatever he chose to do next. He'd not only won them over, but he'd also inspired them to push harder for what they wanted for their own careers.

I knew right then that he wouldn't be packing shelves during the day to take night courses. He might not see it yet, but I was by far not the only person drawn to him. The universe's power of attraction was real. As soon as he put himself out there, more opportunities than he ever dreamed possible would come to him.

Who would I be to him then?

As if my question had reached him, he turned and offered me his hand—his fish-scented, sticky hand—and I took it and beamed a smile up at him because mine was just as bad.

"What do you think?" he asked.

"About?" I'd missed the last thing that had been said.

"Could you see me doing a social media series? Could I be a save-the-ocean influencer? Is there really money in that?"

The interns started talking over each other in their excitement. I hadn't done much with social media, but if passion for a subject equated to success in it, Kal couldn't fail.

He leaned closer, winked, and flexed. "I'd keep my clothes on."

Lynn sighed in audible appreciation.

Yeah, he'd be fine. "You're going to soar."

He pulled me to his side and kissed the top of my head. "Just like you."

Just like me. When he looked at me that way, I felt not just beautiful, but treasured for the first time in my life. Whether this man was meant to stay for a day or a lifetime, I knew I'd be better for our time together. I wanted his time with me to do the same for him. "Call some of those biologists you met. Tell them about your idea and I bet they'll jump at the chance to work with you."

His expression sobered. "Do you really believe that?"

I cupped his face between both of my hands. "Amazing things are about to happen for you, Kal. Try not to forget me when they do."

He gathered me against him, took a deep breath, then bent to say into my ear, "The only thing I'm sure about in all of this is you."

Had we been alone I would have kissed him then, but instead smiled up at him and tried to lighten the mood. "That won't always be the case, but for now I'll do my best to be your rock—your safe haven—your well of wisdom . . ."

He laughed and stepped back. "So that's how it's going to be, huh?"

"Your mentor—your coach—the one you turn to in your hour of need," I continued with humor.

"When I'm big on social media and traveling the world to document all those projects, you'll ask to join me . . ."

"And?" I asked.

"I'll say hell yes, because with you together is always better."

My breath caught in my throat, and I swayed before steadying myself by grabbing the rail of the boat. He'd just said together like he meant it, and I was all for it.

CHAPTER TWELVE

Kal

MONDAY MORNING WHILE Jade slept, I dressed and took my phone and my wallet with me onto the balcony of her apartment. I found the card the red-haired woman had given me after my last show and sent a text: **I'm ready to meet Dominic.**

An answer came almost immediately. **A car is on its way to pick you up.**

I was tempted to ask how she knew where I was, but I was sure I didn't want to know. I headed back inside, showered, wrote Jade a quick note, then tucked it beside her pillow. The last few days had been some of the best of my life. We'd spent a quiet Sunday together. When we weren't making love, we were either napping in each other's arms, swapping stories about our lives, or researching the process of monetizing social media posts.

I'd come to Florida angry and frustrated. Although I still had concerns when it came to my family, I was feeling invigorated, motivated, and optimistic about the future. Jade took the information we'd gathered online and put it in a spreadsheet with goals, then took each goal and broke it into workable tasks. She didn't ask if I was capable of anything she'd put on the list—she believed in me.

I didn't say it, but I was falling hard for her. I wanted to be the man she saw in me and there was nothing I wouldn't do for her. Except wake her.

She knew I was leaving that morning and we'd talked about why. She offered to come with me, but meeting Dominic was something I had to do on my own. I needed to look him in the eye and determine if he was or wasn't a danger to my family. Until I had that answer, there was no way I'd let him near Jade.

I bent and gave her a light kiss that was enough to stir her, but not wake her. If she woke it would only be harder to leave her, so I tucked the blanket tighter around her and headed down to the street to wait for the car. I left my computer and things with Jade because I had no intention of being gone long.

I wasn't down on the street more than a few minutes before a black SUV pulled up and the driver asked me if I was Kal Ragsdale. When I said yes, he opened the back door for me. I looked over my shoulder at the window of Jade's apartment. Meeting Dominic didn't intimidate me. If he was a danger to my family, I'd do whatever was necessary to protect them—even if it cost me my future.

"Is everything okay, sir?" the driver asked.

"I have no idea," I said with a laugh that was directed at

myself. "But hopefully that's about to change." I slid into the back seat of the SUV. As we drove, I did my best to keep an open mind. Everything I knew about Dominic had come from secondary sources: online searches, my mother, my sister, some redhead who claimed she'd known him a long time.

When we pulled through a gate to a private airport my brother's wealth became evident. An army of staff and security met the car. One rough-around-the-edges man in a dark suit stepped forward and offered his hand in greeting. "Marc Stone. I'm here to escort you to your meeting."

"Not everyone would brag about being an escort," I joked. No one laughed—not him, not the men around him. Tough crowd.

He removed his mirrored sunglasses. "Your relationship to Mr. Corisi is slowly becoming known. There's no going back to the life you had before."

"Excuse me?" If he was trying to sell getting on the plane behind him, he was failing miserably. Was he referring to dancing? I'd already left that behind. If anyone thought they could keep me from Jade they had some serious rethinking to do.

"You've been protected since we heard of your existence. To some degree there will always be someone watching your back. They're trained to take a bullet for you if necessary. Try to appreciate them." He replaced his glasses. "Follow me, Mr. Ragsdale."

I did only because refusing to wouldn't have gotten me the answers I needed. "Is the redhead escorting me too?" I had more questions for her.

The man stopped, turned on his heel, and in a low, deadly voice, said, "That redhead is my wife and the only one she escorts who lives is me."

I held my breath. I would bet my life this guy had taken the lives of others. He had that vibe.

Then he smiled. "See, I can joke too. Come on, that was funny, the only thing that would have made it better is if you'd pissed yourself."

I shook my head. "You're fucking with me?"

"A little," he said with a chuckle. "Alethea is my wife, but I don't have to go to battle for her, she's a one-woman battalion on her own." He nodded toward the plane. "You're about to enter a very different world than you're used to, but you're not alone. We're all hoping this works out."

"How long have you worked for my brother?"

"Decades. He took a chance on me when no one else would. I owe him more than I could ever repay. Technically I'm the head of his security team, but he's made sure that I'm also financially set on my own. If you're ever interested in owning a secret bunker, I'm your man."

"Why would I need a bunker?"

"You wouldn't ask that if you saw the ones I design."

Since we were talking frankly, I decided to be upfront with him. "Adjust the focus of your lens back to include reality. I'll be happy to see a regular paycheck coming in again—and that will go toward rent, a car, and school. If I do really well, I might splurge for some healthcare coverage."

Marc didn't say anything for a moment. I could feel him reassessing me. "You really do want nothing from Dominic."

"Oh, I want something." His eyebrows shot up. I continued, "He needs to look me in the eye and assure me that he'll be kind to my mother and sister. They're the only reason I want to meet him."

Marc nodded without saying more and led me onto a plane so large that I felt ridiculous in it. The inside was insanely spacious and ultra-modern. It screamed of self-indulgence and a lack of concern for the environment. "So, what, he's flying me and an entire football team to see him?" I referenced different sitting areas, some with standard seating, some with couches. There was even a conference table.

"Don't tease Dominic about his plane. It's a sensitive subject."

I shook my head as I looked around at it. "So, I'm not the only one who thinks it's gaudy and a monumental waste of money?"

Marc shrugged. "He realizes that, but it also has sentimental value to him. It is being meticulously maintained instead of being swapped out for a newer model."

"Sentimental value?"

"This is the plane he used to kidnap the woman who is

now his wife. They were dating and she was going to leave him, so he flew her off to his private island. Twenty-plus years later they're still together, so who am I to judge?"

"You're joking, right?" He wasn't. "I read that wasn't true."

"You still believe what the media tells you? How about the Easter bunny? Is he real to you?"

I chose a seat beside a window. Dominic kidnapped people? If that wasn't a red flag, I didn't know what was. "Are you trying to get me to not trust Dominic? If so, relax, I already don't."

Marc frowned. "If that's what you think, I'm doing this wrong."

I buckled myself in as if everything was completely normal. A woman came by to ask if I'd like a drink. I declined.

Dominic Corisi wasn't someone people said no to. I'd said no to him from the get-go and was all that stood between him and whatever he planned for my family. What would a man like him do with an obstacle? I decided to pass on ingesting anything until I knew.

The plane's engine started, and we taxied down a runway. Marc took a seat across from me and belted himself in. "This will be a short flight. We're heading to Martha's Vineyard. A little over two hours."

I let out a breath and sat back. "The location doesn't matter."

"Hey, you should cut Dominic some slack. He's trying."

That brought steel to my eyes. "I'm here. If he wants more than that, he'll have to prove he deserves it."

Marc slapped his hands on his knees. "You're enough like him that this will either go really well or you're going to kill each other."

I could have said it would never come to that, but I chose honesty instead. "Either outcome is fine with me as long as my family is safe . . ."

Marc pocketed his glasses and wiped a hand across his face. "That's something Dominic would say." He cleared his throat. "Except, he already considers you family, so he'd be including you in that last part."

I stared him down. "Right now, he's nothing to me. All I've ever had was my mother and sister." *And now Jade,* but I wasn't bringing her into the equation. "That's all I need."

Marc sighed. "I hope this trip changes your mind."

I didn't tell him I doubted it would. We'd both said about all there was to say. I leaned back and closed my eyes. By now Jade would have woken and found the note I left for her.

CHAPTER THIRTEEN

Jade

I WOKE TO my alarm and the realization that Kal was gone. He'd said he intended to reach out to his brother that morning. I'd offered to call in to work, but there'd been no way to know if he'd receive an answer from the number he'd been given.

There was a chance, of course, that Kal had simply gotten up early and gone for a run, but I knew that wasn't the case. The scientist in me marveled at how certain I was of his absence prior to confirming it. I felt that he was gone—it was as simple and as powerful as that.

When I rolled onto my side there was a crunch of paper. I felt around my pillow until I found a handwritten note. **I'll be back as soon as I can. Thank you for understanding that I have to do this. – Kal**

As emotions welled up inside me, I called Nikki and merged Sasha in. "He left," I said with a thick voice.

"Oh, I'm so sorry," Sasha said instantly.

"For good?" Nikki asked.

"I hope not," I said then stopped myself from going

down that dark rabbit hole. "No. He'll be back. He has a few things he needs to do first."

"Such as?" Per usual, Nikki wanted the bottom line first. "And how did things go? How do you feel?"

I propped myself up in my bed. "I realize this is fast, but I think Kal's the one. I've never clicked with anyone the way I do with him."

"Oh, boy." Nikki groaned. "Tap the brakes a little. You just met him."

"That doesn't make it less real," Sasha protested.

"She's still paying off bills from her last engagement."

"Ouch," I said with some bite. "I didn't say we're getting married, just that we had a great weekend together."

Nikki countered with, "And that he might be *the one*."

I had said that and hated how wrong it sounded when repeated back. "You're right. But that doesn't change how I feel."

"And that is?" Sasha asked gently.

"I want this to be real. I don't care if he doesn't have any money or even a job. That's all temporary. Together we'll—"

Nikki cut in, "Jade, listen to yourself. I've seen videos of this guy. I'm not even into men and I understand the lure of him, but what would you say to me if our positions were reversed? What would you tell Sasha to do?"

"I—I—" I'd be saying the same things Nikki was because I loved these women and I'd be worried for them. "Kal isn't the person in those videos. He is so, so much more."

"Okay," Nikki said, "how?"

"Was the sex amazing?" Sasha asked.

I took a deep breath before answering. "The sex was incredible, but that's not how Kal won me over." I told them everything, from how confused he'd been when he arrived a few days ago to the side of him I'd seen when he'd interacted with the interns. "Kal isn't a deadbeat. He's a hardworking, well-read, temporarily unemployed future marine biologist. We came up with a whole plan for how he can parlay his connections into a social media platform that could be financially lucrative. But more than that, he would be a strong voice for activism and fundraising. His depth of knowledge coupled with the way people are drawn to him . . ."

"Sounds like a lot of bullshit to me," Nikki said, and my heart broke a little. "I'd need to see—"

Sasha jumped in, "Actually, *we* don't need to see anything. Nikki, I've seen some of your hookups and from where I'm standing you shouldn't judge."

"Oh, I'm sorry," Nikki snapped, "if I've chosen getting another degree over changing diapers."

"I knew it. I knew you didn't respect my choice to be a stay-at-home mother," Sasha growled.

"I respect your choice, just not your faith in a man who could leave you at any time. At the end of the day, marriage is just a paper. If you don't have some way of supporting yourself . . ." Nikki's voice trailed off. "I'm transferring my own fear that no one will ever love me enough to stay onto the two of you. My therapist said I do that. I told her she was wrong. But I'm doing it right now."

Had we been together in person I would have hugged her. Instead, I said softly, "Just a little?"

"You're still hurting over Daniella leaving to study abroad." Sasha's tone was once again kind and understanding. "It doesn't mean she didn't love you. Or that she won't be back."

Nikki groaned. "I want to say I don't want her back, but I miss her so much it hurts—just as much today as the first day she left."

"Have you told her that?" I asked.

"No," Nikki said quietly.

"Maybe you should," Sasha suggested.

"Sometimes all a woman needs to know is that you're still interested." I voiced Sasha's earlier advice.

Nikki sighed. "It is so much easier to give advice than take it."

Sasha and I laughed. I said, "We can all agree on that."

"Sasha," Nikki said, "I'm sorry if I say things that make you doubt your choices."

"I don't doubt anything," Sasha responded. "I love my husband. We're solid. Things aren't always perfect, and that's okay. Life isn't perfect. I'm not sure it's even meant to be. I don't let that stop me from believing in love and miracles and wishing on candles before I blow them out. We are all blessed with the amazing gift of being able to write the stories of our own lives. So much of that story is up to us to interpret. Sure, Jade might be using great sex with a hot guy to help her heal from a bad engagement, or maybe being single again was where she needed to be so she and Kal could have a chance for something amazing together." After a pause Sasha added, "Maybe Daniella didn't leave you. Maybe she knew she had more growing and learning to do before she chose you. And that's okay."

Overcome with emotion, I said, "Sasha, do you know how much I love you?"

Nikki added, "Me too. Even if I don't always say it."

Sasha sniffed. "You guys are just saying that to see if you can get a pregnant woman to cry. Well, now you've done it, I hope you're all happy."

"It was too easy," I joked.

"It always has been," Nikki added with a smile in her voice. "But if you want to blame the hormones . . . whatever." After a pause, Nikki asked, "So, now it's a wait and see situation for Kal and you?"

I glanced at the ceiling. "That sums it up." When I looked down, I caught the time on the clock beside my bed. "Shit. If I don't hurry, I'm going to be late for work. Gotta go!"

"Have a great day, Jade, and text me if you hear from Kal," Sasha said in a rush.

"Me too," Nikki added. "I want him to be who you

think he is. I mean that."

"I know you do." I didn't expect my good friends to agree with every idea I had or not caution me when they were worried. I wouldn't want a friend who felt they couldn't be real with me.

As I rushed to shower and get dressed, I thought about how Kal and I connected. At the heart of what we were doing I felt we were building a friendship. Although Nikki had backed off, her concerns had been valid. On paper, Kal was a risk.

Sasha had said it best, though. I didn't want to stop believing in love and miracles and wishing on candles before I blew them out. My life was my story. My experiences were mine to interpret. Not marrying Robert wasn't a tragedy.

And falling for Kal felt right.

On impulse, I grabbed the book I'd sent him and took it with me to work. It sat at my desk all day while I went over the data the interns had collected from the BRUVs. It was hard to wait to hear from him, but I understood why Kal had left and what he needed to do before he returned.

I could have been upset that he wanted to face his brother alone, but that fit with everything I knew about him. He put the needs of those he loved before his own. It was what made me want to be there for him with that same loyalty that he was there for others.

If you can hear me, Universe, please keep Kal safe.
And please bring him back to me.

CHAPTER FOURTEEN

Kal

WHEN THE PLANE landed on Martha's Vineyard it was met by another swarm of security. Had there been a photographer I would have walked down the plane's stairs doing a princess wave, but there wasn't one and the mood wasn't jovial.

I took a moment to look around and decided presidents traveled with less protection. "Is all this really necessary?"

From my side, Marc answered, "Your brother has powerful enemies who would love to use someone he cares about as leverage."

"Fantastic," I said with heavy sarcasm.

"Before you judge Dominic, make sure you're proud of every choice you've made."

My head snapped around as my temper rose. "Don't go there."

"When it comes to protecting Dominic, I'll go to whatever lengths are necessary. You want me to care about how you feel too? Prove you deserve it."

It wasn't amusing to have my own words thrown back at

me. "I don't care what you think of me."

"That sentiment is mutual." In a low tone, Marc added, "Come on, we have a helicopter waiting for us."

A helicopter? Why not? My opinion of my brother was lowering with each over-the-top demonstration of his wealth. *You're rich. I get it. We all get it.*

I followed Marc across the tarmac to a waiting helicopter without asking him where we were going. I didn't want to give him the satisfaction of knowing that not knowing was nerve wracking. It wasn't my first flight in a helicopter. Although never one like Dominic's. I was used to being in the same cabin as the pilot, wearing headphones to block out the loud noise. Refurbished helicopters were a tool some divers used to get to places that wouldn't otherwise be accessible. I'd dived directly from the open door of a few into the choppy waters of remote locations.

The plush, soundproof cabin of this helicopter was as foreign to me as every aspect of the trip had been so far. I climbed in and took a seat. Marc followed and sat across from me. When a man popped a head in from the tarmac to ask if I'd like a beer, I joked, "Because you're out of *champagne?*"

"Not at all. Is there a brand and year you prefer?" He listed a few that were chilled and ready.

I frowned, feeling awkward. "No. Thank you."

"Something to eat perhaps? Water?"

"I'm fine."

Marc declined as well.

Once the doors closed the sound of the rotors lowered to a background hum. If this was how my brother lived on a daily basis it was no wonder he thought he could do whatever he pleased. I wondered if, when he shit, there was someone right there to catch his turd and tell him it was marvelous.

Soon after takeoff, Marc said, "Dominic planned a surprise for you."

Since we were headed out over the water, I couldn't help but say, "As long as it's not a long walk off a short plank with me in cement shoes, I'm fine with whatever."

Marc smiled. "We don't do that to *family*."

I met his gaze. "Are you still fucking with me?"

His smile widened. "Maybe."

A super yacht came into view. It had to be over four hundred feet long. Eight or so floors if the windows were anything to go by. There was a pool on one of the decks as well as a helipad. Yachts were a common sight for divers, but nothing like this. Not that I was surprised that Dominic would own such a thing or that he would assume I would be impressed by it. I hoped he didn't ask me if I liked it because that would open a whole other topic, he wouldn't want to hear my thoughts on.

We landed with less fanfare than at the airport. I took a deep breath and mentally prepared myself for whatever was about to go down.

The rotors were off before the doors of the helicopter opened. Marc didn't instantly move to get out so I didn't either. "I know that look and it never appears on your brother's face before he does something he's proud of later."

My smile was more of a baring of my teeth than a reflection of my mood. "I've been clear about why I'm here."

With a shake of his head, Marc led the way out of the helicopter up a stairway to a man who was standing by a rail, looking out over the ocean. We stopped a few feet from him. Only then did he turn to greet us.

What struck me first was how familiar his face looked to me. Although he was older, with some graying near his temples, we had the same gray eyes. His hair was jet black just like mine. Many of our features were similar enough that anyone would guess a relationship by looking at us.

I was an inch or two taller and in better physical shape, but for a man who likely spent most of his time in suits, he was still visibly fit. I met his stare with one of my own. Neither of us spoke.

It could have been the location he'd chosen for us to meet, but the stories my mother had told me of our father came flooding back. My eyes narrowed and disgust filled me as I imagined my mother cowering before someone because she feared the kind of power he wielded—the same kind of power Dominic had. "All I see when I look at you is Antonio and the damage he did to my family."

Dominic stood straighter and held my gaze. "I get that a

lot."

I had expected him to protest that he was nothing like our father, but he didn't. For the sake of my family, I bent a little. "I appreciate everything you've done for my mother as well as my sister."

"It was the least I could do. I was sickened by what Antonio did to your mother."

Looking him right in the eye, I had to ask, "You never knew about us?"

"Not until Judy, my daughter, and Gian, my youngest brother, made a bet to see which of them could be the first to uncover relatives for me."

He appeared to be telling the truth. "And they found us."

"Yes."

I folded my arms across my chest. "And you decided to welcome us into your family? Just like that?"

"You weren't the first surprise sibling I've learned about recently. Antonio fathered Sebastian with my mother's sister. My mother had Gian with another man while she was on the run from Antonio. It's a complicated family tree."

"My other brother. Sebastian who?"

"Romano."

I knew the name but only because most people did. "As in Romano Superstores?"

"That's him."

Great. I couldn't have a normal sibling out there?

"My sister Nicole would have come today, but I didn't tell her I was meeting you. I didn't tell anyone."

That sounded ominous. "Because?"

"I don't know what I think of you yet."

At least he was honest. I respected that. "Because I'm a dancer?"

"Is that what you are?"

"It's what I've done for long enough that it's what I'm known for." I tensed as I spoke. "I'm not ashamed of doing what I had to for my family."

"Good. You shouldn't be. That sacrifice is no longer necessary though. Tell me what you need and it's yours. Tell me what you want—and it'll at least be considered."

I dropped my hands to my sides. "I've heard the stories of how Antonio won my mother over. He drew her in with his money, manipulated situations, then used his power to control her. How do I know you're nothing like him? How do I know you won't hurt my family?"

"I already have." Dominic's expression tightened. "Riley was furious with me, but I'm working on making it up to her."

That didn't sound good. "What did you do?"

This time Dominic was the one to fold his arms over his chest and look defensive. "I was trying to protect your sister."

I leaned closer and repeated my question between gritted teeth. "What did you do?"

He expelled an impatient breath. "She was vulnerable to

being taken advantage of."

I didn't ask my question again, just held his gaze and waited. A dangerous amount of anger was already welling inside me, and I regretted not calling Riley before coming to see Dominic. I should be hearing about this from her, not him.

"She's already forgiven me."

My silence was my power and I used it to keep the upper hand.

Dominic continued, "I'm here on Martha's Vineyard to choose the location for a carnival we're planning for this upcoming weekend. Gavin intends to propose to Riley. She loves carnival games, so we thought—"

"That's not going to happen. I haven't even met Gavin."

"It's happening. And you should be there."

I shook my head and took a step back. "Hold on, if my sister is getting engaged this weekend, I'd know."

"We're surprising her."

"We?"

"Gavin and I."

"No."

Another silent standoff. I didn't like that he knew more about what was going on in Riley's life than I did. Several moments passed before I asked, "What did you do that upset my sister?"

He cleared his throat. "I paid off anyone who asked her out, made it difficult for her to work as a paid bridesmaid, and used the instability at Gavin's company to test his loyalty to her." He threw both hands in the air in frustration. "Before you say it, I know I went too far."

He didn't paint a pleasant picture. I demanded, "So, I'll ask you again, how different are you from Antonio?"

His eyes burned with a torment that gave me pause. "On my worst day, not a whole hell of a lot—but I have never and would never hurt the innocent. I keep my rage and my demons far away from my family. My place in hell is secured, but not because I haven't tried to make up for what I've done—what our father did. Both weigh heavily on me."

These were the scars Alethea had described. Dominic was as damaged as she'd claimed. That still didn't make him someone I wanted around my family. "Why would you pay off anyone who was interested in Riley?" Was he trying to isolate her?

"When you have money it's difficult to know if someone wants to be with you because they genuinely like you or because they want something from you."

"You tested them."

"Yes."

"And they all failed."

"All except Gavin." A faint smile pulled at Dominic's lips. "He told me to shove off."

"Good." At least Gavin had that on his side. I might end up approving of him.

"And the job? Were you trying to get Riley to depend on

you?"

Dominic looked side-swiped by the accusation. "No. Of course not. Weddings are difficult to secure without being obvious. I didn't feel they were safe for her."

"And my mother? How much have you been manipulating her?"

He shook his head. "So far she wants nothing to do with me."

That rang true. "What about the man she's with—Hamilton?"

"He doesn't even like me." Another small smile. "This weekend will win them both over. It'll be perfect—every last detail."

"My mother is as hard to impress as I am. She doesn't care about your money."

He cleared his throat again. "I understand that, but I've invited people who know me well. My hope is that she'll see I am not a devil. Or if I am, I'm at least one that only wants the best for her."

"That wouldn't be enough for me." I wasn't sure what to say except the truth. "I don't know what to believe about you."

"What would be enough?"

"I don't know." I looked around. "You and I are very different people."

"Are we?" He lowered his arms. "When I was my worst, and I'm not proud of who I was back then, all I really wanted was to know what had happened to my mother. I sold my soul for the power to force my father to tell me the truth." He pinned me with a look. "What did you trade your soul for?"

My voice was hoarse when I answered, "My mother's health."

"I was angry for so long it nearly consumed me."

For the first time I felt a connection to him. "I've battled that myself."

"Then I met Abby." His expression softened. "She saw something in me . . . and became a beacon, calling me back from the edge."

I understood that as well. "I met someone special recently. She makes me believe I can be better than I've been."

"Marry that one."

I coughed. "We're just starting out and I'm currently in no position to ask anyone to tether their line to mine."

"Piece of advice? Just be good to her." He waved a hand at the yacht in general. "None of this matters with the right person. In fact, I believe Abby loves me in spite of it."

I relaxed a little. "Did you really kidnap her?"

He rolled his eyes skyward and shrugged. "Can you kidnap someone who wants to go with you?"

I chuckled at that. "Why do I think you'd be in trouble if she heard you say that?"

He smiled. "I'm in trouble with her all the time. I still stumble sometimes, but she's right there to help me get back up and try again."

"Stumble?"

He made a face. "The less you know the safer you are."

What the hell does that mean? Something in my expression must have given my thoughts away because he added, "I don't take down anyone who doesn't come for me or mine first—not anymore, anyway."

I couldn't tell if he was serious or not. "So you've earned those enemies."

He shrugged. "Some. Others are a byproduct of my success. If you want people to like you, don't do too well in life. People love to see the underdog rise, but then they love to see him fall again. I haven't fallen, and that has won me more adversaries than anything I did early on." There was a lull in the conversation that he ended with a change of topic. "What do you think of this ship?"

Considering the fragility of the truce we'd unofficially called, I didn't want to say.

He continued. "It's dual purpose. On one hand it has a movie theater, a bar, a gym, several bedrooms, and an entire private floor dedicated to the owner. The thirty or so staff have quarters below, but access to their own Jacuzzi."

The owner? Was it a new purchase of his that he was excited to share the details about or was he once again trying to impress me? "Sounds—expensive."

"What would you say if I told you that it doubles as a research vessel? Its prior owner lent it more than once to the

US government to use. It can comfortably hold two smaller boats in its hull as well as a remote-control submarine with a variety of mechanical arm attachments. I'm not into that kind of stuff, but I did enjoy testing it out."

"Did you just buy this yacht?"

"I did. I bought it for y—"

The sound of one helicopter taking off so another could land interrupted what he was going to say. We both turned to watch the exchange and Dominic appeared as surprised as I was. He motioned for me to follow and headed toward the stairs that led to the helipad. "It's Abby. Someone must have told her I was meeting you."

I almost laughed at that. "*You* have a snitch?"

He paused halfway down steps and said, "Oh, so many of them. I used to find their loyalty to Abby over me irritating, but if people are going to disappoint someone, I'd rather it be me than her."

It was an unexpectedly beautiful thing to say about his wife that left me not knowing how to respond. He turned and I followed him the rest of the way to where we waited for the passengers of the helicopter to exit. A tastefully dressed, middle-aged woman ushered a younger woman and lanky boy past the swirling rotor blades. As soon as they were clear, the helicopter departed, and the original returned and cut the engine.

The younger woman rushed over. "Dad!" She gave him a hug, then stepped back and smiled at me. "Kal, I'm your niece, Judy, and I'm here to save you."

I offered her my hand. She shook it vehemently. "Thank you?" Her smile was so warm and open I found myself smiling back. "I didn't know I was in danger."

"Not in physical danger." When she shook her head, her long ponytail swung back and forth behind her. "My dad comes on too strong. Like this boat. It's too much, right?"

She was a bit much, but not necessarily in a bad way. "It's a lot."

"I told him not to buy it for you. I told him it was too big of a welcome-to-the-family gift."

Wait. What? That had to be a joke.

She flounced. "I keep telling him he wouldn't have so many issues if he'd take my advice."

"Judy, stop," the woman behind her said as she stepped forward with an easy smile. "Kal, I'm Abby, Dominic's wife. It's a pleasure to meet you." She pulled her son forward. "And this is Leonardo, our son."

The boy who looked younger than ten shot me a pained smile. "Hi, Kal."

"Nice to meet both of you."

"You're enormous," Leonardo said. "Is that natural or did you use steroids?"

"It's not polite to ask people things like that," his mother said quietly.

"All natural," I answered smoothly. He wasn't the first to ask me that and likely wouldn't be the last. "A lot of hours in the gym went into these." I raised an arm and flexed for him.

Leonardo raised his own thin arm and frowned at it. "I don't look like much now, but considering my gene pool, I could conceivably turn out like you. My dad is old and he's still muscular."

Dominic leaned over and ruffled his son's hair. "Old, huh?"

Leonardo shot him a guilty smile. "It's not a judgment call, just a fact."

Dominic laughed and met my gaze. "These are the people who keep me humble."

They certainly had an effect on him. Any aggression or anger I'd sensed in him earlier was gone. It was fascinating to watch him transform to a family man before my eyes.

"I like them already," I said, earning smiles all around.

Abby greeted Dominic with a kiss then a wag of her finger. "You. Didn't we just talk about this? You promised to give him space and take things slowly."

Dominic wrapped an arm around her waist. "*He* reached out to me."

"I did." It was true and his kids were watching. Any man would have helped out.

"And I didn't tell him the boat is for him." He gave his daughter what was an attempt at a stern look. "If he says no now, it won't be my fault."

Judy put her hands on her hips. "It won't be mine either. Mom, tell him this is the kind of gift that scares people off."

I looked around before saying, "You're probably joking, but to be clear, I would never accept a gift like this."

"I'll take it," Leonardo said as if it were the last mozzarella stick on a plate that no one else seemed to want. "This is the one that comes with a submarine, right?"

"Good memory," Dominic said with a smile.

"Is the submarine a Nautilus Vas or a Triton? Or did you splurge for the Atlantis 9?"

"That would definitely have been a splurge," I said with a hint of sarcasm that went right over Leonardo's head.

"It would have been, for sure." He was quite serious when he explained, "Given the choice, though, I'd go with the deep-sea Triton. The company has set new records using it to explore the Abyssal and Hadal zones. Oh, man, I'd love to go there."

"When you're older," Dominic promised.

Leonardo rolled his eyes. "He says that about space too."

"Being you is rough," I joked.

"Sometimes." Leonardo looked down then met my gaze again. "You really don't want this yacht?"

Abby cut in, "Judy, why don't you and Leonardo go check out the submarine for yourselves." She gave them a look. "Don't get in it. Don't even touch it. Just go see which type it is."

"Mom," Judy protested. "I'm the one who found Kal. Leonardo can go see the submarine with Marc."

"Excellent idea." Abby called out, "Marc."

He appeared. "Yes?"

"Please take Judy and Leonardo below to see the submarine. Do not let them touch anything."

"I'm not a child, Mom," Judy said in a low voice.

Abby's expression didn't change. "Then I won't have to ask you to go twice."

Judy looked like she might argue that as well but didn't. "Come on, Leonardo. The *adults* want to talk."

When they were out of earshot, Dominic said, "She's a handful."

"No idea where she gets that from," Abby added with a straight face.

He hugged her closer to his side then shot me a look. "My wife is all talk. She adores me."

"I do," Abby said without hesitation, then smiled at me. "But that doesn't mean he's not a handful as well. Sometimes he goes too far."

I needed to see her take on a situation, so I said, "Like what happened with Riley."

Abby looked up at Dominic and sighed. "Exactly." Then to me she said, "I fell in love with this man when I saw what a good person he was under all that growl. He would do anything for the people he loves."

Dominic's chest puffed with pride.

His wife added, "He just has a tiny problem with respecting boundaries."

He didn't look upset by her share. After giving her a kiss

on the side of her head, he said, "You do realize I can hear you, right?"

"That's my hope," Abby answered with a sweet smile. "And, Dom, before you say anything, you know Leonardo is too young for his own yacht."

"I didn't buy it for him. I bought it for Kal."

I had to interject. "I meant what I said. I don't want it."

Dominic gave me a long look. "Because you don't want to owe me."

I conceded that with a tip of my head.

"Gifts don't come with strings." He sighed. "I bought it because you love the water."

He's testing me. That's what this is to him. My mood took a nosedive. "No, you wanted to know if you could buy me. You can't. I'm not interested." I still couldn't look myself in the mirror when I thought about how I'd let him pay off my contract. I would have thanked him for that, but I couldn't get past the self-disgust that welled in me each time I thought about it.

"That's not what this is," he said harshly.

Some of my anger with myself might have been reflected in my tone. "If it walks like a duck and quacks like a duck, it's a duck." I knew it was low to add, but I couldn't stop myself from saying, "How much did you give my sister? What did you buy her with?"

"Dominic," Abby said when she saw Dominic's expression change. She implored, "He doesn't know you. He needs time to."

Dominic straightened to his full height and glared at me. "No, I'm done." He leaned toward me. "I've been good to your mother and Riley, better than you've been lately."

That had me growling back, "Don't you dare imply that I've been anything but there for them."

"Really? Then why am I the one who has met Gavin? Riley is about to get engaged to a man you don't know. I call her daily to check on her. When was the last time you spoke to her?"

"Shut up." I sucked in a breath as his words hit me like a punch below the belt.

"Dominic, this isn't helping." Abby looked from him to me and back. "Dom, tell him you didn't mean that."

"But I did." Dominic threw his hands up in the air. "I refuse to be the villain while everyone else pretends they're perfect. You know what, Kal, get off this boat. I'm officially ungifting it to you. Go back to Florida. Sulk. Say whatever the hell you want about me. I don't care."

"I don't understand you. Is this some kind of twisted game for you?" I demanded.

"Yeah," Dominic snapped. "That's what this is—a fucking game. And so much fun I just keep playing it. Get out of here. You remind me too much of everything I don't like about myself."

I pointed to the water around us. "Should I start swimming?"

He swore and walked away.

Abby lingered. "His feelings are hurt."

"I'm sure that's what that was."

She sighed and walked away saying, "I don't know what to do with either of you."

CHAPTER FIFTEEN

Jade

WHEN MY WORKDAY ended without hearing from Kal, I told myself it had been unreasonable for me to think he'd have time to call. I declined an offer from a coworker to grab something to eat together. If Kal called, or better—returned—I wanted to be there.

I headed back to my apartment, tidied things up, made myself some soup, then a tea, and curled up with a novel from my favorite author. Unable to enjoy the book the way I normally would, I decided to end the day early. I placed my phone near me on the bed and made sure none of the settings were on silent.

Sleep wouldn't come. I tossed and turned, cycling through worrying and reassuring myself. It was late.

What if things had gone badly with his brother—really badly, and he was being hurt or held against his will? As the last person who'd spoken to him and likely the only one who knew where he was, wasn't it my responsibility to alert someone?

There was a chance that things had gone so well that he

simply hadn't had time to call me yet. Maybe he and his brother had a few laughs followed by a few drinks and he was passed out on his brother's couch.

Or he simply didn't want to talk to me.

That last thought had me turning over and fluffing my pillow with a punch. No, that wasn't it. I hadn't imagined the kind of connection Kal and I had. It had been intense and real.

He'll call and when he does, I'll feel foolish about worrying.

He thanked me for understanding that he had to go.

That's not a man who doesn't care about my feelings.

He'll call.

Or wake me with a knock on the door because he can't wait until morning to see me.

I did eventually fall asleep and woke to my alarm in what felt like mere minutes later. I checked my phone—nothing. I forced myself to get up, get dressed, and head to work. It was the first day since I'd started my job that I could say I didn't enjoy being there.

Halfway through the day, unable to stop myself from doing it, I sent Kal a text: **Are you okay? How did it go?**

I stared at my phone for a pathetically long time before I acknowledged that he wasn't going to answer me—at least not right then. Eventually, I put my phone away and pushed through the day at work. The interns asked if Kal and I wanted to join them for a drink that night. I declined without telling them that I couldn't ask if he wanted to go because I had no idea where he was.

When I returned to my apartment after work, I was tempted to call Sasha and Nikki, but I already knew what they would both say. Sasha's optimistic take wouldn't resonate with how I was feeling, and I wasn't ready to have what was left of my hope challenged by a reality check from Nikki.

Kal's laptop was still on the coffee table in my living room. It drew my attention repeatedly even as I made my dinner. I frowned at it while munching on my salad. *He wouldn't have left his laptop if he had no intention of coming back.*

He would have taken it with him if he didn't trust me with it.

But he did trust me, just like I should trust him.

I washed my dinner plates and placed them on a rack to dry then headed back to the living room. With a sigh I sat in the chair where Kal had sat the last time he'd used his laptop.

Leaning forward, I laid a hand over the closed top of it. *If the situation were reversed, he would probably be worried just like I am. Worried enough to search one of my computers for a sign that I was either okay or in trouble?*

I forced myself to stand and leave the room before I did just that. A hot shower made me feel a little better. Checking my phone for a message from him confused me again.

Why? What would keep him from taking a moment to tell me he's okay?

Did he lose his phone?

That was a possibility. In the age of no one knowing anyone's phone number, it was highly unlikely he would know mine. I checked the messages on all of my social media sites—even checked my email in case he'd used that to contact me—nothing.

I told myself not to overthink it, but worry was slowly being replaced by anger. Everything he'd said, every kiss, every touch . . . had led me to believe he cared about me. Men who cared, called—period.

He was worried about his family. It was possible he'd gone straight from seeing his brother to checking in on his mother and sister. Forgetting to call me and then not answering my text wasn't considerate . . . but he did have a lot on his mind.

That night I lay in bed staring at the ceiling of my darkened bedroom. I couldn't believe—couldn't wrap my mind around the fact—that I hadn't heard from him. Unless everything I'd shared with him had been a lie, there was something wrong.

It was well after midnight when I gave up trying to fall asleep and headed back into the living room. *Everything I want to know might be right on his computer.*

I picked up the laptop and took it with me to the couch. It wasn't password protected which made me feel guilty, but not enough to stop. A file on its desktop caught my attention immediately: **For Jade**

There's nothing wrong with reading something he wrote for me. I opened the folder and gasped when I saw how he'd titled the folders within it: Journal for Jade, Photos to show Jade, Places I'd like to take Jade. He'd told me that thinking of me had helped him through some dark days. *So, he meant that, at least.*

I settled back onto the couch and started to read the journal. He'd included such detail in the description of each excursion that I felt I was there with him—especially after looking over the photos that accompanied each entry. The depth of Kal's understanding of those projects was impressive, but his admiration for each of the experts was the real beauty of the writing.

It didn't hurt that he'd started each entry with: **Jade, I wish you were here. Today I . . .**

He had to care about me. So where was he?

An email icon caught my attention. *I won't read more than I have to.* Proof that he was okay would either be there or it wouldn't be.

It wasn't.

Outside of my email to him, most of his inbox was spam. I should have stopped there, but I clicked on one of his social media accounts. It loaded and opened; no hacking necessary since the passwords had been auto saved to his computer.

Regret came hard and fast.

He hadn't made a recent post. On one hand that made me feel better even as it increased how worried I was for him.

I clicked on the message box. It held thousands and thousands of unread messages. As I read through them, my heart sank. So many were from women offering to hook up with him. *Thousands of women.* Most of the messages were in English. Many had photos attached. Some included images of women doing things to themselves that I could only assume was meant to turn him on.

Thousands.

I opened another of his social media apps and found the same. More women. Some men. More elicit offers. More photos.

I should have stopped there. I told myself to. I couldn't. One after another I opened his accounts until I was physically sick from it and had to close the laptop.

So much for making me feel better.

I replaced the laptop on the table and kicked the table away from me. How stupid could I be? He wasn't hurt and in need of rescue—he was with one of those women. Or maybe not, maybe he ran into one of the few women on earth who hadn't written to him and decided to fuck her.

When will I learn?

How many times do I need to be in this place before I stop trusting men who don't deserve it? Nikki was right. Kal is nothing more than a rebound guy.

I called in to work the next day, but not because I was ill as I claimed to be. I needed a day to mourn . . . and heal.

I finally have a life I love.

I refuse to let a man . . . any man . . . ruin that for me.

We're over, Kal Ragsdale. I refuse to give you space in my head or my heart.

CHAPTER SIXTEEN

Kal

FROM THE BEACH outside the hotel room I'd rented in Cape Cod, I read over Jade's message again. **Are you okay? How did it go?**

I didn't have an answer to that, no different than the day before when it had first come in. Not an answer I felt like texting anyway.

I'm not okay. Not at all.

Of all the scenarios I'd imagined when I'd headed off to confront Dominic, I hadn't considered that he would best me simply by being a better brother. Everything he'd said before he'd stormed away had been spot-on true.

While he'd been calling Riley daily to see how she was, I'd been sending her calls directly to voicemail. Nearly two months had gone by since I'd spoken to her or our mother.

Why? I'd stopped talking to Riley when all of our conversations began to revolve around her wanting to get to know the Corisis. Our mother's fear wasn't enough to stop her. Warnings from me weren't either. Somehow, we'd gone from being each other's biggest cheerleaders and practically being able to read each other's minds to lying to each other. She'd told me she wasn't sneaking off to spend time with the Corisis and I'd told her I didn't care either way.

I'd cared. I'd cared so much it made speaking to my mother excruciatingly painful. Conversations with her began to always turn to how concerned she was for Riley and how helpless that made her feel.

Simply because I was hellbent on completely fucking up, I'd also handled hearing from Gavin Wenham badly. He'd called to tell me I needed to be there when he proposed to my sister.

I wasn't proud that I'd let his tone put me on the defensive. If I could do the conversation over, I would put my anger aside and ask him if he loved my sister. I hated that I'd ruined an opportunity to get to know his character. My temper had started to rise when Gavin offered to send me money if that was what was stopping me from coming. I'd lost the battle with my pride when he'd told me this was my opportunity to show my sister that I cared—as if I hadn't done that for most of my life. The call had ended with him asking me flat out if I'd go and me saying I'd think about it.

I wanted to head home and fix the situation, but I didn't know how. Dominic was right to judge me for that. I'd failed the people who mattered the most to me. In the end, all I'd done was leave them vulnerable to him. Lately everything I said and did made it worse rather than better for my family. If I went to Martha's Vineyard, I'd probably fuck that up as well.

And Jade? What did I have to offer her? I wasn't the man she thought I was—and pretending I could be would only lead to me disappointing another person I cared about. *Sorry, Jade, you're better off without me. Trust me, end things now before I have time to really fuck up.*

A lone man in a suit caught my attention as he made his way across the sand toward me. *Dominic?* I rose to my feet. If he'd come for round two, I was up for it. I couldn't see how that would make things better, but on the other hand, things couldn't get much worse so—*Bring it on.*

As he drew closer, I realized it wasn't Dominic, just someone who looked a lot like him. I took a wild stab and said, "Sebastian."

He stopped a few feet from me, pocketed his hands, and rocked back on his feet. "Kal."

"Did Dominic send you?"

"Abby actually." He looked around. "Could we talk somewhere less—sandy?"

So, this was my other brother. I looked him over from his expensive leather shoes to his tie. "I appreciate that you—"

"No, you don't, but I've been there. You feel like shit and the last thing you want is someone coming in and telling you that things will be okay because you can't imagine a way they ever will be again."

"That about sums it up."

He glanced from me down at the sand then took a seat in

it. "You have no idea how many times I told my brothers to leave me alone." When he looked up at me there was enough emotion in his eyes that I couldn't walk away. "They never did. So, sit your ass down. I'm not going anywhere either."

I blinked a few times then sank into the sand a foot or two away from him but facing the ocean. I had no idea what to expect from him, so I held my silence and waited.

He cleared his throat. "Do you want to talk?"

"I don't fucking know you."

He looked around then met my gaze. "I don't see anyone else here, do you?"

Ouch. True. If he was trying to make me feel better, he was failing. "Listen, the whole supportive brother act is beautiful, but I have all the family I need."

He stared me down. "Are they here? Did I miss them?"

"Funny, only I'm not laughing, so maybe not that funny."

He looked back at the ocean and sighed. "Have you ever wished you were dead? Not in passing—not just once. Have you ever looked in the mirror and hated the man you saw so much that you felt removing yourself from everyone's presence was the kindest thing you could do for them?"

His words spoke to a dark corner of my soul. "I'm not suicidal."

"Self-destruction isn't always about jumping off a bridge or holding a gun to your head. I used to drink myself numb and hope I wouldn't wake up."

The crash of the waves calmed the storm in me enough for me to say, "I've been in that place."

"And?"

"And I pulled myself out of it."

"And you will again."

I glared at him. "You don't know me or anything about my life. No offense, but I don't have any fucks left to give when it comes to this conversation."

He smiled at that. "Things that bad?"

I turned to look out over the ocean again. "Why are you here?"

"Did I mention that my brothers never left me—no matter what I said to them—no matter how self-destructive I was? They couldn't fix what was wrong in me, but that didn't stop them from making sure I knew I wasn't alone. You're not alone, Kal."

It was tempting to want to have the brothers described, but I didn't believe it was possible. "Biologically we might be related, but that's all we have in common."

"For now." He let those words hang in the air.

A wave of rage came and went—leaving me feeling defeated and not entirely sure what or who I was angry with. "I fucked up. I thought I was taking care of my family, but I wasn't. Not the way I should have. Even now while I'm sitting here trying to figure things out, I'm fucking things up more."

"I've been there." Sebastian inhaled. "It seems like a

lifetime ago, but I had a wife who loved me with all her heart. I thought I knew what being a good husband was, but I didn't. I thought giving her a nice house and an easy life was love." He cleared his throat. "I should have been with her the day she headed off to get an ultrasound for our baby. I wasn't. There was a business meeting I felt I had to go to. Not a day has gone by that I don't regret that decision."

"What happened?" His pain was so intense I held my breath.

"I lost both of them to a car crash." He slapped his hands on his knees. "So, I know what it feels like to fuck up. Something died inside of me. It took me a long time to forgive myself."

"And now?"

"I've been blessed with a second chance. I have a wonderful wife, five amazing children, and I can finally look myself in the mirror again."

"It's a nice story."

"It could be yours as well, but it starts by facing whatever it is in you that you hate. That's the dragon you have to slay."

"It's not that easy."

"I know it isn't. It took me years. Thankfully, I had help and a reason to keep going. Heather and Ava believed in me even when I'd lost faith in myself."

"Who are they?"

Sebastian smiled. "Heather is my wife, but she and Ava

came as a package deal. Ava is her daughter and now officially mine as well. I've also been blessed with incredible parents."

"Even though your mother was also with Antonio?"

Sebastian's expression tightened. "We don't talk about him, but yes. Turns out my mother was once just as human and fallible as the rest of us. She was dating Antonio before Dominic's mother, Rosella, married him and moved to the United States. There's a lot of years of anger and pain on that limb of our family tree. We're all finally in a good place now, though."

"Did you grow up with Dominic as your brother?"

Sebastian smiled. "Noooooo. Which was probably a good thing because our relatives in Italy used to call him the devil. It's a long story."

And one I'd read about. "They don't call him that anymore?"

"They confused him with Antonio and that ended once they got to know him. Dominic is—an acquired taste. We all are, I suppose. He and I both faced challenges. The difference between us is that he faced his battles alone. I never had to. Even when I felt unlovable, there were people making sure I knew they were waiting for me to come back to them. He didn't have that."

I thought about my mother and sister. I had that. "Not even his sister, Nicole?"

"When Dominic left to look for his mother, he left Nicole with his father. For a long time, she couldn't forgive him for that, and he felt he'd failed her. He hates that he wasn't there for her when she needed him."

The last part of our fight made sense to me then. "He told me I remind him too much of what he hates about himself." I'd left Riley just like he'd left Nicole.

"You didn't meet Dominic at his best. He was still reeling from disappointing your sister. He takes things like that hard. I believe he wanted to redeem himself by working things out with you. From what I heard that all went south when Abby and the kids arrived to save you from him. Dominic has been cast as the villain so many times, it must be frustrating and that's why he lashed out at you."

Our interactions that day made more sense after hearing that. "I didn't help the situation. When he said he was there for my family more than I've been lately—"

"It hurt to hear because you felt it was true."

"Yes, and I said some things I shouldn't have."

"My brothers and I often invite Dominic out with us so he can see how healthy sibling relationships work. We joke. We fight. We make up. Life goes on. No matter how angry we are, we'd still drop everything for each other if one of us were in need. He's never had that and it's what he craves more than anything else."

I shook my head. "Why did he buy me that yacht?"

Sebastian shrugged. "I'm not a psychologist. I don't understand half of what Dominic does, but maybe he just doesn't know another way to show people he cares, at least not at first. With him, it's a process."

"Did you get a yacht?"

"Money isn't one of my issues."

Yeah, I could see that.

After a moment, he asked, "What are you messing up by taking time out to think?"

I tapped my phone and showed him Jade's last message before returning my phone to my pocket. "I should have answered her on Monday when she sent the message." I ran my hands through my hair. "She's been wonderful to me. I've read the message about a hundred times. I've even started to respond a few times, but . . ." Did I really want to say it aloud? On the other hand, keeping it all in my head wasn't taking me anywhere good. "Things used to make sense. I knew who I was—even if who I was wasn't someone I liked. I don't know anymore. Everything is changing so fast. My sister is getting engaged to a man I've never met. My mother is dating now. We used to be so close I knew what they had for breakfast most of the time. How did we lose that?"

"You tell me."

I wanted to lay the blame at someone else's feet, but when I looked back, the fault was mine. "I got frustrated and angry—mostly with myself—so I pulled away."

"Did that make anything better?"

"No, Captain Obvious, that appears to have been a bad

decision."

Rather than snapping back at me, I could have sworn Sebastian hid a smile behind a fist before he responded. "My father is much better with advice than I am, but have you considered that you might be stuck in a pattern?"

"Pattern?"

"You deal with problems by pulling away . . . hiding isn't the right word for what I'm trying to say but isn't that essentially what you've been doing with your family . . . and isn't it what you're doing with your female friend as well?"

"I'm not *hiding*," I said forcefully, then looked at my recent behavior and corrected, "I'm totally fucking hiding." Not out of fear, but because I didn't want to face how both situations made me feel about myself. Shit.

"It does seem that way."

I sighed. "Why? I face most things head-on."

"No one is like that all the time. Your mother hid you and Riley from Antonio."

"She had no choice."

"Exactly. Pulling back from a situation she couldn't control was how she survived and how she kept you safe. She taught you to do the same."

"That's not healthy."

"Then stop it."

Why I hadn't called Jade back finally made sense to me. "I'm starting over from scratch. Jade's in a good place . . . finally happy after having a rough time. I don't want to pull her down."

"Then don't."

I nodded. "That's why I'm staying away from her."

"Solid plan—as long as you don't care about her."

"I do. I care about her—a lot."

"Then answer her. Break the pattern before it breaks you."

Break the pattern before it breaks you.

He made that sound so easy, but how do you stop something you weren't even aware was a part of you? You face it head-on. *I need to do better.* "I want to be with her."

"Then get off the beach and go to her." He rose to his feet and dusted the sand off his trousers. "Come on. This is a place we all visit sometimes, but you can't stay here."

He might have been referring to Cape Cod, but I guessed that he meant the place my thoughts had taken me. I stood as well, brushed the sand off my jeans, then fell into step beside him. "Hey, Sebastian."

"Yes?" He paused to look at me.

No more hiding. No more holding back. "This whole having brothers thing takes some getting used to, but thanks."

He clapped a hand on my shoulder. "Anytime."

CHAPTER SEVENTEEN

Jade

HAIR TIED IN a sloppy knot on top of my head, I closed my eyes and sank neck deep into the bubbles I'd added to my bath. I was tired, but in a good way. Not only had I cleaned my apartment and my car, but I've boxed all traces that Kal had ever been in my life into a cardboard box and put it just inside my door. Tomorrow, if I still hadn't heard from him, I'd put it outside the door.

I was angry with myself for taking the day off work over someone who very likely wasn't putting a single thought into me. The lack of consideration some people had for others still shocked me, but I told myself it shouldn't. Life had been teaching me that lesson from day one when my mother had chosen a lifestyle over me. My problem was I refused to believe that it could happen again.

At the very least, I needed to take a break from men until I finished paying my grandparents back. I also should warn Sasha that building Daniella up in Nikki's head was setting her up for more pain.

Breaks were better when they were clean. Not a heated

storm-off. A betrayal that couldn't be forgiven hurt but was final. Despite the difference in length of time I'd known them, I preferred how things had ended with Robert over Kal.

Even when I added in the embarrassment of having to contact everyone who my side had invited to tell them the wedding was off. I'd choose going through that a hundred times over waiting and worrying that Kal might be dead only to face that he didn't care enough to call me.

At least Robert had groveled and tried to fix things with me. He might not be able to be monogamous, but I did believe him when he said he was sorry. He would have still married me. He swore he could do better. On some level, by his own definition of it anyway, he did love me.

That wasn't a love I could live with.

Kal hadn't said he loved me, but he'd said he cared. He'd sat with me, planned out how a future together would look, and let me believe.

A sound caught my attention—was someone knocking on my door? The water sloshed as I hastily got out of the tub. I threw a towel around me, found my phone, and checked my security app for video.

Kal.

I sat heavily on the corner of my bed. *No.*

He had a wrapped gift in his hand.

I tapped a button on my app so he could hear me. "No."

He was looking into my doorbell camera. "I'm sorry,

Jade."

"Sorry would have been enough Tuesday morning or even this morning. You let me worry for days that something might have happened to you—you could have been dead for all I knew." My voice thickened with emotion at the end. "If you wanted to prove to me that I mean nothing to you, you chose an effective method."

"I was thinking only of myself, Jade. I'm sorry. I swear it won't happen again."

I shuddered. "Robert said those same words to me. Exactly the same words. I didn't believe him either."

He had nothing to say to that. *Good.* While I was feeling strong, I said, "I have something for you."

Uncaring that I was only wearing a towel, I swung the door open and pushed the cardboard box toward him with my bare foot. "Here's your stuff."

I shouldn't have looked him in the eye because when I did desire slammed through me. We might not be a good match for each other, but my body certainly hadn't gotten that message. It was so acutely aware of him, so hungry for his touch, I ached.

His nostrils flared, his eyes burned with the same hunger I was fighting, but he looked as happy about it as I was. "I brought you something." He held out the wrapped gift.

"I don't want anything from you."

"I wish I could say the same." He leaned in and I flushed from head to toe. "You have no idea how much you matter to me."

Trying to stay strong, I said, "Because you've shown me I don't."

"No, I've shown you that there are parts of me that still need work. I pulled away from my family when I couldn't deal with not knowing what they needed from me. I pulled away from you when I realized I'd failed them."

I retightened the towel around myself. I understood the first part. It was the same reason I didn't call home to check on my grandparents even though I loved them. I didn't know what they needed from me, but I knew that somehow, inevitably, I always disappointed them. The second part? I didn't know how to feel about that. "Things didn't go well with Dominic?"

"Do you want to hear about it?"

I did, but inviting him in was also inviting the possibility of more and . . .

"We don't have to talk tonight." He bent and placed the gift he'd brought for me next to the box of his things, then straightened with the box in his arms. "I'm still renting a room at—"

Judge me all you want but I grabbed him by the arm, dragged him inside, and closed the door behind him. He dropped the box. I dropped my towel.

He lifted me so my legs wrapped around his waist. I wound my arms around his neck, and we kissed like waves crashing into the shore. There was no holding back, no way we could even if we wanted to. This was primal, cosmic, a storm one couldn't hold off—only ride out and hope they survived.

Between kisses, I whipped his shirt up and over his head. He kicked his shoes off then shed the rest of his clothing without putting me down. Each movement caused muscles to ripple between my thighs and me to hang on tighter.

He trailed kisses down my neck, over each of my breasts and back to my mouth again. Whatever anger I had left in me was suffocating beneath wave after wave of pleasure. My body was in glorious overload. His hands were strong and sure. Our kisses tasted like a fulfillment of everything I'd thought was impossible.

Nature didn't care why he hadn't called me.

I was eager for him when the tip of his cock slid across my wet sex. More than eager. I met his first thrust with one of my own—slamming him deeply into me. He moved to brace me against the wall. Together, we went wild. I dug my nails into his lower back. He pounded into me relentlessly, gloriously—deeper and deeper as I soared toward climax.

We kissed. We cursed.

He told me he'd missed me.

I told him to shut up.

I didn't want to think about why giving myself over to the pleasure of him might not be wise. No one else had taken me so completely. It was impossible to think of anything beyond how good he felt in me, all around me . . .

He slowed his pace, bringing me to a tearful, wild orgasm then bringing me there again, all while holding his own pleasure back. I was still shaking and clinging to him from my second climax when he groaned and came.

Still wrapped around him, he carried me to the bedroom and lowered me to my feet beside the bed. A moment later, he returned with a warm washcloth. I took it from him and wiped myself down before turning to toss the cloth behind him onto the tile in the bathroom. Regret for not using a condom would have to wait until I sorted other things out. We stood there without speaking or touching for several minutes, then I picked up a pillow and swung it at his head. "I'm so mad at you."

He blocked the pillow with a hand. "I know."

I released the pillow and he let it drop to the floor. "What just happened does not mean you're forgiven."

His eyes burned into mine. "Okay."

I frowned. "It's not okay." I pushed at his chest until he took a step back. "Nothing about any of this is okay."

He simply held my gaze without speaking.

Tears filled my eyes. "You weren't supposed to be like Robert."

"I'm not." My only consolation was that he looked as hurt as I felt. "I fucked up, but not the way he did. I would never cheat."

The memory of all the offers he had waiting for him on his computer came back to me then. "You've given me no reason to believe you."

He nodded slowly. "I haven't shown you my best. Even tonight, I should have apologized and left."

Shame nipped at me. "I ruined that plan."

He brought a gentle hand to my cheek. "You didn't ruin anything. I did. You have been nothing but good to me. You deserve much better than I've given you."

"I do." I folded my arms across my stomach protectively. "I was finally happy. You are not allowed to come in here and destroy that."

His face tightened as if my words had caused him physical pain. "That's the last thing I want to do." I told myself the anguish in his eyes was well deserved even while I fought back the desire to wrap my arms around him and tell him it would all be okay.

I needed to stay strong. "You hurt me."

"I know."

"I don't know if I can forgive you."

He let out a slow breath.

I continued, "Or trust you again."

"Do you want me to go?"

I should have said yes. What we'd just shared should be chalked up as goodbye sex. Really, really good goodbye sex. "No," I said in a hoarse voice. Without meeting his gaze, I walked to my bureau and began to dress. "But put some clothes on."

I didn't turn to see how he felt about that but did hear

him walk out of the room. Would he keep walking straight out the door and out of my life? I had no idea.

Feeling less vulnerable, dressed in a T-shirt and shorts, I headed out to the living room. Kal was dressed again, shoes and all, standing beside the cardboard box. When he looked up, he said, "Jade—"

I raised a hand in plea for him to stop. "Don't apologize again. It won't change anything."

He lifted and dropped a shoulder. "What *do* you want?"

I rubbed my hands over my eyes. "I want you to have not blown me off for days when you knew I was waiting to hear from you and worried." His silence confirmed that that was an unrealistic request. I sat in one of my chairs next to the couch and pulled my legs up in front of me, wrapping my arms around them.

He moved to sit on the couch beside my chair and waited.

I took a deep breath. "What happened when you went to see your brother? You did go to see him, right?"

"I did." He ran a hand through his hair and sat back. "He flew me up to Martha's Vineyard then I took a helicopter to a yacht he had offshore."

"And?"

"He told me I remind him of everything he doesn't like about himself."

"Harsh."

"Somewhat deserved. Most of what I was angry with him

about was not his fault. He didn't hurt my mother. I was the one who stopped talking to my family when things got complicated. I lost my temper when I realized he knew more about what is happening back home than I do, but that has more to do with me being a shitty brother and son than Dominic being a danger to anyone."

Normally I would have told him he was being too hard on himself, but I couldn't comfort him while I was still upset.

"We argued and I flew back to the mainland. I thought about calling my family. I thought about calling you . . ."

"But?"

"Have you ever gotten yourself so tangled up on the inside that you just want to be alone?"

I had. Still, I had to ask, had to hope I'd recognize a lie if he told me one, "And that's what you were . . . alone?"

He held my gaze. "Yes. I rented a place in Cape Cod and . . . hid." He said the last word with disgust. "I'm not proud of that."

One confession deserved another. "I looked through your computer and your messages. I'm not proud of that either."

He tipped his head to the side. "My messages?"

"On all of your social media accounts." My hands fisted. "You get so many offers to hook up . . . the temptation must be overwhelming."

He leaned forward in his chair. "I don't even read them.

They don't matter."

I waved a hand in the air. "They never do."

He frowned. "I'm not Robert."

"No, you're my rebound fuck after him."

He sucked in an audible breath, and I couldn't look him in the eye. That had been a low blow and I regretted saying it as soon as it came out of my mouth, but I wasn't ready to apologize for it.

Neither of us spoke for an awkward amount of time. Eventually, he said, "I should go." He stood and waited.

I fought back a strong desire to stand and throw myself in his arms. "Kal?"

His eyes met mine and I couldn't tell which of us was more miserable. "Yes?"

"Don't forget your box."

He rocked back on his heels then picked it up. He lingered there for a moment as if he might say something more, then silently walked to the door. At the door he bent to also pick up the gift he'd brought me. He placed it on a small table near the door then let himself out.

I didn't move, didn't let myself beg him to stay. I just sat there, blinking back tears until I forced myself to stand, walk over to the door, and lock it.

We really were over—and it was for the best.

No matter how wrong it felt.

CHAPTER EIGHTEEN

Kal

I SAT IN my rental car outside of Jade's apartment sorting through layers of regret. I couldn't go back in time, but there had to be a way to show her to give me another chance.

I took a deep breath.

Even if she forgave me, I was barely better than the man who'd disappointed her—and I meant the me from a few days earlier, not Robert. I was still broke, unemployed, and at odds with my family. I kept thinking she deserved better, but I didn't yet have better to offer her.

You're my rebound fuck. She hadn't said it because she meant it. No, I'd hurt her, and she'd said that to hurt me. That was a cycle I understood too well.

All that had stopped me from snapping something back was what Sebastian had said, "Break the pattern before it breaks you."

I drove to my hotel, carried the cardboard box of my things into my room, and placed the box on the bed. Everything I'd left at her place was in it, right down to my toothbrush. I took my laptop out to see if the screen was cracked from when I'd dropped the box. It wasn't and I smiled at the irony. The only thing that wasn't broken was the one thing I would know how to fix.

I pulled out my wallet, removed the credit cards from it, and laid them out on the counter. "Which one of you has enough credit left on you to get me home?"

None volunteered so I did things the old-fashioned way: I booked a cheap flight and tried each of the cards until one worked. My sister was getting engaged. No matter how much I didn't want to leave Florida yet, or how much time had gone by since we'd spoken, I couldn't miss a life event like that.

I needed to begin to fix what was broken—not just with Jade.

Flight booked and paid for, I decided to tackle another issue. The spreadsheet Jade had made for me was detailed and a great place to start. Step one was to reach out to the marine biologists I'd already connected with. I smiled at the list she'd started for me based on the ones I'd written in the margins of book she'd sent me.

I glanced back at the box. The book was there as well. Not a good sign.

When I returned to my computer, I saw the folder I'd made for her and wondered if she'd read through that and what she'd thought as she had. I knew she'd read over my message boxes and, after Robert, I could understand why. I didn't need to open them to know what she'd seen in there.

In the very beginning of my career, I'd found those messages exciting, easy pickings. Time had proven how meaningless they were. A person really could have too much sex. A younger me wouldn't have believed that possible, but there was a tipping point to gluttony—where overindulging led to self-loathing. Walking away from that lifestyle hadn't been about changing who I was, but rather raising my standards both for myself and for those I spent time with.

The situation I found myself in was similar. Only instead of indulging in blowjobs from strangers, I'd allowed myself to put my needs above those of the people I cared about. Some people might feel empowered by always putting themselves first, but I loved my family.

And I love Jade.

It'll take time, but I can be the man she needs.

Knowing that I was the only one who could make the changes I needed to, I took out my phone and texted a number I had before. **Have Dominic call me.**

A few minutes later, my phone rang. "What do you need?" Dominic asked in a harsh tone.

I put my pride to the side and said, "I'm sorry. I really am grateful for all you've done for Riley and my mother. Also, thank you for releasing me from my tour contract."

"You're welcome." There was silence, then he said, "And I am the last person who should judge how someone treats their sister."

I cleared my throat. "What do you say we wipe the slate

clean and start over? I want to be there when Gavin proposes to Riley."

"You belong there. I'll send a plane—"

"No." I softened my tone and added, "I already have a ticket back. All I need are the details."

"Everyone is staying at my place on the island."

"Your house?" I didn't know if I was ready for that.

"I renovated a beachside hotel. It's all private suites. You should stay there with us. Your sister will want you to."

"Okay." He was right. It would also give me more time with my mother and this man she was dating. "Thank you."

After a moment, Dominic asked, "Is this as hard for you as it is for me?"

I chuckled. "I hate this stage."

"Me too. A clean slate is a good idea. You were never a little prick, and I never lost my temper with you."

"Hold on, who are you calling *little*? I don't do anything halfway."

He laughed at that. "Something else we have in common." After a pause, he added, "Riley will be really glad you're there."

"It'll be good to see her."

"How about your lady friend? Will you bring her with you?"

I remembered what Sebastian had said to me on the beach about how Dominic was still learning how to be a brother. Was I any better? Riley and I had always told each other everything and that had given us a strong bond. "Jade's not currently speaking to me. I took a little too long to get my head straight after I met you."

"You left her hanging."

"I did."

"Have you tried apologizing?"

"Did that."

"A gift?"

"Delivered, even though she didn't want it."

"What's your plan?"

"To get my shit together, turn my financial situation around, and go back to her as the man she needs."

"That's a horrible plan that ends with her moving on to the next guy while you figure things out."

"I'm not kidnapping her."

He laughed. "Wow, do you think my whole game relied on that one move? Trust me, Abby wouldn't still be with me if that was all I had."

He and Abby did have a good relationship track record. I sat down, propped my feet on the coffee table, and asked, "Sure, why not, lay some of your wisdom on me."

"First, send a car for her—"

"All I can afford is an Uber."

He made a sound in his throat, then said, "I'll hire a driver for you."

"Dominic."

"What?"

"I don't want your money. I don't want you to solve my problems."

"Then what do you want?"

I took a moment to ask myself that same question. "Sebastian came to see me in Cape Cod, and we talked. The only family I've ever had was Riley and my mother. When he described how things were with his brothers and him—I wished I had that."

In a deeper tone, Dominic said, "Sebastian's a good man."

"Yes. I feel like I could call him at midnight, and he wouldn't hang up on me . . . that I could share the good and the bad with him and he'd get me. That's where I'd like to get with you."

"I'd like that."

"You're successful. I wouldn't mind running some business ideas by you and hearing your thoughts on them. Just advice, nothing else."

"I have time now."

I picked up my laptop and began to go down the list of tasks on the spreadsheet. He stopped me periodically to ask questions and give suggestions. By the end of the conversation, I could see how he'd gotten as far as he had. He had a keen sense of how to attack a problem on multiple levels. "I want to have made some progress on this before I see Jade again."

"Then you don't have time to build up a social media

following. Write up your proposal and present it to people with the funds to invest in this endeavor. Money opens doors."

"I don't—"

"It doesn't have to be my money. When the cause is a worthy one, the money comes. You want to save the oceans? Sell me on how you could do that. One way. Focus on one goal and sell it to me."

"Offshore buoys for Catalina." I explained the devastation that was left behind by anchors and how simple the solution would be—all that was lacking was the funding.

"Okay, now who do you know who is working on something related to that?"

I named a marine biologist I'd met in Thailand who was working on a similar offshore project for several island countries. I also told him about the angry master diver I'd toured offshore Catalina Island with.

Dominic said, "Reach out to both of them. Tell them what you'd like to do for Catalina and about each other. Line up people in the press who might be interested in the story. Take your idea to Netflix, Disney, anyone who will listen. Knock on every door. One will open. When it does, present your plan, right down to how you've fanned media interest for the project."

"That does sound like a good plan."

"It's only as good as you make it. Do I think you can do it? Yes. Will you? I have no idea."

Because I've done nothing lately to inspire faith in me. "I needed this, Dominic. Thank you."

There was a smile in his voice when he said, "Anytime."

CHAPTER NINETEEN

Jade

WHEN I ENTERED the office the next day, I was handed a mountain of data to sort through and enter. I would have preferred the distraction of being out at a site, but there was a price to be paid for taking a day off. Had I actually been ill, a day in the office would have been a welcome additional day to heal.

Another sleepless night had me feeling a bit ragged. After Kal had left my apartment, I'd done my best to be okay with how we'd ended, but his gift had sat there next to the door, taunting me.

Somewhere around two a.m. I'd made the mistake of opening it. Had he bought me jewelry I could have said he didn't know me. I'd never cared for that.

Had it been a coffee mug, I would have scoffed and said he hadn't paid enough attention to my preferences to know that I was a tea drinker.

All the box contained was a folded piece of paper. At first, I'd thought it might be a letter from him apologizing, but it wasn't that either. It was handwritten information on how to join a volunteer group that was diving at an artificial reef in Pensacola in a couple of weeks. Participation in the dive was by invitation only and Kal had arranged a slot for me if I was interested. All I had to do was confirm and I was in. Beneath those instructions he'd written a brief overview of the dive. The lead researcher was gathering data on PCB levels in the marine life surrounding a purposefully sunken military vessel the government had already spent $20 million on cleanup.

I'd read about the ship. Originally it had been applauded for very quickly attracting and harboring a variety of marine life. Despite following EPA disposal guidelines, the ship had contained a significant amount of toxins that had shown not only a negative impact on the environment but also a health risk to humans. The dive was part of an ongoing study of the prolonged effect of sinking decommissioned military equipment.

It was the most thoughtful gift I'd ever received and one I didn't know what to do with. On one hand, participating in something like that, with the team that was leading the dive, was a once in a lifetime opportunity. On the other hand, how could I enjoy it knowing that Kal had arranged it?

And how long would it be until the thought of him stopped feeling like I'd just lost my best friend? Robert and I had dated for a couple of years, and I didn't miss him. *What is wrong with me?*

"Oh, wow, you look awful," Pete said.

"Thanks," I said as I sat at my desk.

"No, seriously, I wouldn't normally say anything, but you're looking like you shouldn't be here today."

An unlikely save came from Lynn, "Lay off the compliments, Pete, before you give her a big head."

"Sorry," he said. "But look at her. We could have covered for you today if you weren't ready to come back."

"There is *nothing* wrong with me. I'm fine." There was snap to my tone, one that surprised both interns.

They took a step back. "She doesn't look feverish," Pete said.

"We're here if you need us," Lynn said, and they both fled my area.

I took advantage of their departure and dove into my work. I loved data in general, so even when the findings weren't significant, they were enough to keep my interest. The problem was that each time I surfaced to take a break my mood plummeted.

The office emptied for the day, but I stayed, trying and failing to think of anything but Kal. If I removed Robert and my residual certainty that all men are cheaters, what was I angry with Kal about? From our prior conversations I knew that Kal had felt torn between his loyalty to his mother and his inability to stop his sister from going against their mother's wishes. I knew how worried he'd been about meeting Dominic and now I knew that their meeting hadn't gone well. He'd rented a place in Cape Cod and hidden? To think? Alone?

Outside of the messages I'd read that were evidence of how readily available female company was to Kal, did I have any reason to doubt his version? Had he actually done anything to warrant me calling him a rebound fuck and tossing him out?

When I boiled down the reason for my anger, a lot of it was due to how worried I'd been for him. I'd also been hurt because I'd taken his silence as a lack of care for my feelings.

But what if . . . what if his pulling away hadn't all been about me? What if he'd just needed time to clear his head before returning to me?

My face warmed when I remembered how heated that return had been. I'd never understood people who claimed to accidentally have had sex with someone. Prior to Kal, passion had always been something controllable—like sailing on quiet waters. Kal was the storm that came out of nowhere with high waves that crashed over the deck. Scary. Over-whelming. Exciting.

I didn't want to go back to how things had been before him. I didn't want things between us to be over. I took out my phone and texted Kal: **I'm sorry about the rebound comment.**

He texted back almost immediately. **I understood that you were angry.**

I shouldn't have gone through your computer.

I have nothing to hide, so search away. Considering how we met I get why you'd have doubts.

I know you're not like Robert.

Good.

I held my breath and typed: **Would you want to meet for dinner tonight?**

My heart sank when he didn't immediately answer. I let my breath out in a gush and gave my cheeks a smack. When it came to Kal any coolness I may have had fell away.

I'm flying to Boston. In fact, I'm just about to board a plane.

Oh. I scrambled to know what to write to that. **Visiting your family?**

Yes. My sister is getting engaged tomorrow on Martha's Vineyard. I'm here for the weekend.

That's great. It was—even if it meant I couldn't see him, I knew how much his family meant to him. **You wouldn't want to miss that.** Would he return to Florida afterward? I'd already asked him to dinner, I wasn't ready to sound needy as well. I waited for him to say, "I wish you were here . . ." but he didn't. I did have something I needed to say. **Thank you for the gift, Kal. That's an amazing opportunity. Do you plan to join the dive as well?**

I would, but I'm working on something right now that's time sensitive.

Oh. **Well, it was really considerate.**

I was hoping you'd like it.

I did. I do.

Hey, I'm boarding my next flight. Text later?

Sure.

I replaced my phone in my bag and dove back into work.

I told myself I needed to finish entering the data before I left. The truth was, I didn't want to go home. Too many questions waited for me back at my apartment—along with too many memories.

I couldn't lie in my bed without thinking of how good it had felt to have Kal there with me. The shower only reminded me of laughing our way through our first time washing each other down. Would I ever look at my living room without my face warming from memories of him carrying me through it and how exciting not being able to make it to the bedroom felt?

Yeah, I didn't want to go home yet.

I took out the paper he'd sent. His handwriting was big and bold, just like his stage persona, but what he'd written was sweet and thoughtful . . . the Kal I'd welcomed to my bed. My opinion of him the last few days had been pretty low. He'd avoided me as well as his family, it was easy to judge him, but was I any better?

My grandparents may not have always said what I wanted to hear, but I'd never lacked for food or clothing. They'd been at the sidelines of every sport I'd ever played. No, they hadn't coddled me when I lost, but they'd always bandaged me up and sent me back in the game. More than anything, they'd raised me to get back up every time I fell.

I'd craved physical affection and praise, which explained the lure of Robert. Right out of the gate, he'd said he loved me. I'd found comfort in how often he held my hand or put an arm around me. Although I considered myself a strong woman, I'd traded my independence and dreams to have him. Love shouldn't come with that price tag.

In the quiet of the empty office, I reflected on the relationships in my life and the role I played in each. There had been so many signs that Robert wasn't faithful to me, but I hadn't wanted to see them. There were an equal number of signs that my grandparents loved me. Why had it taken hearing about Kal and his family for me to see that?

It had been over a month since I'd called home. I'd told myself separation was good for all of us. They could take a rest from worrying that I'd fail, and I'd have a break from trying to convince them that I wouldn't. I thought about how not hearing from Kal had made me feel and realized I'd been wrong.

Since they detested texting, I called them. "Hi."

My grandmother answered. "Jade?"

I laughed with little humor. She asked that every time like my ID didn't come up on her phone. "That's me. How are you, Grams?"

Instead of answering me, my grandmother called out to my grandfather. "It's Jade. She wants to know how we're doing."

In the background I heard my grandfather ask a slew of questions: Was I still in Florida? Did I find a primary doctor yet? How was my car holding up around all the salt air? Did I take his advice about getting it treated for that yet?

I smiled because nothing had changed. "Everything is fine here. I was just missing you."

"She's missing us," my grandmother repeated for the benefit of my grandfather. He said something I didn't hear, then she added, "No, I haven't asked her anything yet. You're standing right here. You would have heard me. Well, then go get your hearing aid." To me, she said, "Your grandfather is in deafness denial. Or he just doesn't want to hear anymore. I'm not sure which."

"I'm sure it's denial," I said to be kind although it could be a case of both. "I would have called earlier, but things were busy here . . ." It was just an excuse and it didn't land well. At least when Kal messed up he owned it. I needed to do the same. "I'm sorry, Grams, I needed time to sort myself out."

Her tone softened. "Of course you did. We understood. I wanted to give that Robert of yours a nut twist for how he treated you." My grandfather said something in the background and my grandmother said, "Yes, that's what I said, I wanted to give him an iced tea. Does that even make any sense?" In a lower voice she added, "I'm beginning to think his deafness is a gift. I can finally say whatever I want to."

That did make me laugh. "Hold on, you've been *holding back*?"

"You have no idea." After a pause, she added, "I'm not one to celebrate anyone's pain, but did you hear about the little bridesmaid who broke you and Robert up?"

"Technically, Robert—" I decided I wanted to hear the story more than I wanted to get into semantics. "What happened to her?"

"Oh, they were hot and heavy—in public too. Please, no one needed more proof that she was a whore. Your cousin Carol . . . well her mechanic's son went to a party where she and Robert were practically having sex in front of everyone."

"If Carol's mechanic's son saw it—that's all the firsthand accounting I require."

"I know your grandfather and I encouraged you to try to work things out with Robert, but Carol said he broke that little bridesmaid's heart by hooking up with someone else the very next night. I call that karma."

I do too. Why people thought a cheater would never cheat on them had always been a mystery to me.

To my grandfather, Grams said, "Yes, I called a llama because that's how I've always handled situations. Parker, if you don't get your hearing aid—"

"Grams, can I speak to Gramps?"

"Sure, but good luck."

"Jade." My grandfather didn't sound old or confused. His voice was as strong as ever.

"Are you deliberately trying to annoy Grams?"

He chuckled. "I can neither confirm nor deny that."

Leaning back in my chair, I laughed. That was what I loved about the two of them. No, they'd never been the type to read me a bedtime story, but when they bantered, they were a hoot. "I miss you."

Without skipping a beat he asked, "Did you find a doctor yet? Don't wait until you need one."

It wasn't what I yearned to hear from him, but maybe people weren't meant to fit into the little boxes we thought they should. Maybe we could love each other despite that. "I will do that this week. I promise."

"Good. Same thing with your car. Get ahead of the rust. And I'm not there to check your brakes or oil. You know you have to check both on a regular basis."

Distance helped with perspective. At home, when he'd spoken to me that way, I'd thought he doubted my competence. I was beginning to think he was simply worried for me—no different than I had been for Kal. "I'll find a good mechanic and stay on top of that. If you have a minute, I'd love to tell you about my job here."

"Hang on, I'll put you on speakerphone so we can both hear."

"Oh, *now* you can hear?" my grandmother challenged.

I smiled. Although we'd spoken since I'd moved to Florida, those conversations had consisted mostly of them telling me that personal responsibility didn't end just because I'd moved away and that I still had to pay them back. I'd impatiently told them that I was aware of that but also thought they might want to know that I was okay. The conversation hadn't gone well after that.

This time, I refused to get defensive when they asked me

if I thought there was any job security in my entry-level position. I assured them I was working my butt off to insure there would be. I told them about my volunteer work as well as the upcoming opportunity I had in Pensacola and what an honor it was to be invited. I left off how that had happened.

"Volunteering doesn't pay the bills," my grandmother said. "You'd be better off with a second job."

I sighed. Old insecurities nipped at me. Why, why was nothing I achieved ever enough? Instead of asking that or ending the conversation, I decided to take a different approach. This time I'd focus on what they'd done right instead of wrong. For me—my sanity. "You raised me to take care of myself. I don't worry if I can make this work, I know I can—I'm resilient like that." Neither of them said anything and for a moment I thought perhaps the call had dropped. "Grams?"

Her voice was thick when she answered. "That's all we've ever wanted for you, Jade. You don't know how much I prayed you'd be stronger than your mother was. She was our baby, and we did everything for her because we thought that's what good parents did. She was soft because we failed her."

Tears filled my eyes. Was that what they truly believed? "My mother was an adult when she had me. Her bad choices were *hers*, not yours."

"You can say that, but you didn't change her diapers. You didn't pry her off your leg the first day of school. Addy was a beautiful soul. She was so kind, so smart. To see that drop away when she started doing drugs. And then to watch helplessly as she self-destructed. Pray you never bury one of your children, especially not due to what she chose. You're never the same."

I could only imagine—and I didn't want to. "You didn't fail her, and you definitely didn't fail me." I took a deep calming breath. "I have a good life and you gave that to me. Just because I moved away doesn't mean I'm not grateful. There were simply better opportunities for me here and I love knowing that I'm making a difference."

My grandfather cleared his throat. "Your grandmother and I were thinking about getting a condo down there. We've been putting aside the money you've been sending for your wedding. It's enough for a deposit on one. We could be snowbirds. And if we put your name on it, the condo would be easy enough to leave to you when we . . . you know."

I wiped tears from the corners of my eyes. "I love the idea of you getting a place down here, but I don't need my name on it. You guys are going to be around for a long time."

"Don't argue. You can't live day to day," my grandmother stressed. "Financially this makes sense. It'll gain equity while we're alive and then you'll have that when we're gone. The house here isn't worth much, but it'll be yours too."

Emotion clogged my throat. Although they didn't say the words, what was this if not love?

"The wedding payments will cover the mortgage payments for now," my grandfather said. "As long as you can afford to keep paying us back."

"I can," I said and inhaled deeply. "I'll contact a Realtor."

"No," my grandfather said firmly. "First get yourself a primary doctor and a mechanic. Call us when that's done and then we'll talk about the condo."

A little teary, but smiling, I said, "Okay." I glanced out the window and was surprised that it was already dark. "I have to go, but I love you guys and I'll call soon."

"Not after eight. You know we like to go to bed early," my grandmother said.

"I remember."

"And have the tread on your tires checked," my grandfather added. "I hear it rains a lot down there. You don't want to hydroplane."

"I will. Good night."

They ended the call without responding, but that didn't dim my smile. The current state of my life was a matter of perspective—and my perspective was changing in a positive direction. I'd never had a parent who wrote little notes of encouragement and stuck them in my lunchbox, but my grandparents had never been late to drop me off or pick me up.

It couldn't have been easy for them to take on the responsibility of diapers and late-night feedings when they'd thought their baby days were over. I'd never felt that their home wasn't mine as well. I'd always known they'd raised me to not head down the same path my mother had taken, but I'd never really grasped the pain behind their motivation.

It gutted me that they felt they'd failed their daughter. If my mother was on the other side watching, she had to be proud of her parents and as grateful for them as I was.

I thought about Kal and his family and hoped he found a way past his issues with them. Ours were certainly different situations, but I understood the importance of family and how being in a bad place with them could shake a person's foundation.

Enough to need a couple of days alone? Absolutely.

Kal had mentioned that he was working on a few time-sensitive things. Were they family related? I wished I'd asked.

I shut down my computer, grabbed my purse, and headed to my car. A movement of someone in the shadows had the hair on the back of my neck standing on end. Although my office wasn't in a bad neighborhood and the parking lot was lit, I was the only one around and that had me regretting I didn't have Mace in my purse.

I hastily crossed the parking lot to my car and breathed out in relief when I locked the doors. A quick glance around revealed nothing worthy of the adrenaline rushing through me, but I couldn't shake the feeling that someone was watching me.

I started my car and drove from the parking lot onto the

road. In my rearview mirror I saw a car start up. *I'm being paranoid.*

Remembering advice I'd once read about personal safety, I took a right turn. The car took one as well. I took another right turn. Once again, although farther back this time, the other car did the same. When I took a right for the third time, I held my breath and kept glancing backward over my shoulder. It appeared and then pulled over as if whoever was in it had realized I knew they were following me.

Drive to a police station. That's what I need to do. I tried to remember where one would be. When I couldn't, I voice-activated my phone and asked for directions to the nearest police station.

As the directions were loading, my phone rang with a number I didn't recognize. I ignored it and took a left-hand turn. When the car didn't appear behind me, I laughed nervously. *I've watched too many movies.*

My phone rang again. Normally spam calls annoyed me, but my nerves were frazzled and talking to someone, even if all they wanted to do was sell me something, sounded good. I took a right onto a main road that went in the direction of my apartment. "Hello."

"Jade Tremblay." For a salesperson, the caller had a deep, authoritative voice.

"Yes."

"This is Dominic Corisi, Kal Ragsdale's brother."

I swerved then righted the car. Everyone knew the Corisis. Kal's brother was that Dominic? The Corisis were American royalty. Kal wouldn't have left something like that out, would he? Thinking back, his references to his brother had been vague. I'd watched a documentary on them once and everything Kal had told me about his mother fearing his father would make sense if his father had been Antonio Corisi.

"Are you still there?" he demanded.

"I'm here. Sorry, it's been a long day."

"Everything okay?"

I let out a shaky breath. "I guess. Yes, sorry. So, you're Kal's brother. He's told me a lot about you, just not your last name."

"All good?"

I made a noncommittal sound.

He grunted. "Anyway, I realize your relationship with Kal is none of my business, but I also believe in cleaning up the messes I make. When I spoke to Kal, he mentioned that you had a falling out after he came to see me."

I kept my eyes on the road and my hands tight on the wheel. "You spoke to Kal . . . recently?" It sounded as if they'd reconnected.

"Yes, he called me."

"So, you're okay with each other now?"

There was a pause before he said, "Yes. We are. But this isn't about us, it's about you."

"Me?"

"If Kal and I hadn't . . . argued . . . he wouldn't have needed a few days to think, and you would still be together. You should be talking to him. He needs you in his corner."

"Did he say that?"

"He cares about you. What I want to know is if you feel the same."

"I'm sorry?"

"I can't pay you off. I promised to not do that again."

"Pay me off?"

"I don't want to threaten you. Everything I've read about you makes you sound like a nice enough person."

"You've read about me?"

"What's the disconnect here? Should I speak slower?"

I shook my head to clear it as my ire rose. "I can usually keep up just fine, but you're not making any sense. Where would you have read about me?" Maybe social media? I didn't post that much.

"None of this is important. Just answer one question. Do you care about Kal? And when I say care about, I mean do you want me to fly you up this weekend so you can be there for when his sister gets engaged?"

My mouth dropped open. "I—I—if Kal wanted me there he would have asked me."

"No, he wouldn't have. He has this stupid idea that you deserve better than who he is today. If he's not good enough for you when he's down, you're not good enough for him when he rises."

Somewhat insulted and more than a little confused, I said, "I never said he wasn't good enough for me. I do care about him, but I don't need you to fly me anywhere and I wouldn't want to go anywhere he didn't ask me to be."

"That's not how you get anything in life. You don't sit around hoping stars align and people say exactly what you want them to when you want them to. Do you want to be with Kal or not?"

"Yes?" I said in a squeak.

"Then act like it. What is standing between you being together this weekend? Money? I'll cover the trip. Don't feel you have the right clothes? I'll send you for a spa day and a shopping spree. You can have a whole makeover on me. Is it the lack of an invitation? I'm inviting you, right now."

My eyebrows rose. "Why would I need a makeover?"

"I have no idea. Some women like that. You're probably fine as you are."

It could have been the adrenaline leaving my body from when I'd thought I was being followed, but I imagined Dominic in a conversation with my grandparents and I laughed. Amusement replaced irritation. "Dominic, do you mind if I call you Dominic?"

"Go ahead."

"Kal and I spoke before he left. He could have invited me, but he didn't. I'm okay with that. We'll talk when he comes back." *If he comes back. If he was working on things that meant he couldn't attend the dive in a couple of weeks, did that mean I wouldn't see him for weeks?*

"I'll send a car for you."

I laughed. "I just said no."

"No, you said you're okay with waiting for him to return to you. Is that what you accept from life—whatever's *okay?* I'd hope a future sister-in-law of mine would have higher standards."

"Future—I do have high standards."

"Not in my book. If I want something I go after it. I don't settle."

"I don't set—" I stopped as I realized that's exactly what I had done with Robert, with my job back home, and it was what I was doing again by letting Kal choose when we'd see each other again. "I do, but not anymore. Dominic, I do want to be with Kal."

"Then let's get you up here."

I hated to ask. "Is it . . . is it a formal event?"

"Some of it. I can have someone call you to make sure you have everything you need."

"Okay," I said tentatively. "I'm not going to be intruding on something personal, am I?"

"Jade, he wants you there. No, he needs you there. Just don't mention that I arranged this."

"Don't mention it? You're the one who invited me. What would I say I was doing there?"

"Yeah. I'm going to take heat for this, but Judy was right—I shouldn't have led with the super yacht. Sometimes

I come on too strong."

My hands were shaking as I parked outside my apartment. "Maybe just a little." I scanned the area and tensed when I saw the car from earlier parked down the street. "Dominic?"

"Yes?"

"I think someone's following me. I mean, legitimately, tailing me. I'm going to call the police."

"Don't. I knew I should have sent one of my own guys down there. Do me a favor and walk over to the car."

In a high-pitch tone, I asked, "You want me to what?"

"He needs to hear this from me."

"He?"

"My guess is it's Bartel's son. We use Bartel's security team sometimes when we need a few extra men. Lately Bartel has been grooming his son to take over. The kid is book smart, not street-smart. He needs to know he shouldn't be seen when he's watching someone."

"Why would you have someone watch me?"

"Do you know who I am?"

"Yes."

"People know that Kal is related to me. That makes him a possible target. He cares about you. Are you following this?"

"Yes." And my heart was racing again. "Am I in danger?"

"Not tonight. Not from the idiot I want to have a few words with. Walk me over there."

"Okay." I got out of my car and walked down the street

to the vehicle I'd run from earlier. The man behind the wheel looked fresh out of college. I handed him my phone "It's for you."

The man's face turned bright red. "Sorry. I know. I didn't mean to." Something Dominic said silenced him. I felt bad for him until a huge smile lit his face. "You'd do that? Thanks. Yes, I'd love that. Absolutely. Do you want me to stay on the job? Awesome. Thanks. This really means a lot to me. I'll tell her."

The call ended before he returned the phone to me. "Sorry about the scare. I'm still learning."

"That's okay." *I mean, what else could I say?*

"Mr. Corisi wanted me to tell you that he'll send a car for you tonight. I'll be flying up with you. He offered to send me through the same training his personal team goes through—Marc Stone's boot camp. My dad is going to freak-out when I tell him. With that kind of training, I could take our company to the next level. Thank you for convincing Mr. Corisi to not fire me."

"I didn't. He's just nice like that?"

The young man stepped out of his car. "I'll walk you to your door."

"Thank you."

At the door he was still smiling. "I'm going to Massachusetts by Corisi invitation!"

"Me too," I murmured, let myself into my apartment, waved to him, then closed the door behind me and repeated, "Me too."

CHAPTER TWENTY

Kal

M Y FLIGHT FROM Boston to Martha's Vineyard was canceled while I was making my way to the gate. After a frustrating hour of attempting to find an alternate flight only to discover they were booked solid, I was tempted to call Dominic, but my pride didn't allow that. I was already grateful to him for the advice he'd given me.

The Catalina buoy project was now more than an idea. I'd spent the last two days contacting marine biologists I knew who had worked or were working on similar projects. They'd been intrigued and open to the possibility of participating in a documentary if I could land one. Then I contacted the master diver I'd taken the diving tour with. He was onboard although not optimistic that it would actually happen. Endless calls to people in traditional media as well as online environmental influencers and I could say I'd at least created interest in the project. Contacting potential production companies for such a documentary proved frustrating. Not surprising, but they weren't eager to talk to someone who cold-called with an idea, not even when I said I'd drummed up interest in the project.

I was about to table the effort until after Riley's engagement when I received a call from Bilboa. One of his friends had mentioned my project to him and my idea for filming the process. He gave me the name of someone he worked with at Netflix and told me he'd have the guy call me. After that, it would be up to me to sell the idea, but Bilboa said he would love to do a cameo appearance because anchor damage to reefs was a global concern.

I'd knocked and a door had opened.

It was exciting enough that I'd wanted to call Jade, but we hadn't been on speaking terms until she'd texted me right before I'd boarded the plane to come North. An opportunity like the one that might be coming my way was too big to be shared in a text—and I wanted more than just a possibility of success before I told her.

Jade had trust issues. I understood why, but something she said haunted me: "You've given me no reason to believe you."

Words carried little weight with her—she'd been let down by them in the past. I needed to go to her with something concrete, a win that would show her I was dedicated to our shared passion and to her. I might not currently be able to afford to return to school, but that was a situation I was finally confident I could turn around and still make a positive impact on the environment while doing it.

More pressing than that, though, was my need for an

alternate method of getting to Martha's Vineyard. I checked the ferry schedule, estimated travel time by car, booked an online ticket at a dock over an hour away, then ordered a car. Thankfully the only luggage I had was a backpack.

On my way to the dock, I realized I hadn't told my family that I was coming. I'd meant to. I'd put those phone calls on my mental to-do list, but somehow the time had gotten away from me and I hadn't.

More accurately, I hadn't known what to say or where to start. My mother and I had had so many conversations about how neither of us wanted anything to do with the Corisis. Should I start off by asking about my mother's new boyfriend? The one who was the father of the man who was about to ask my sister to marry him—even though I knew nothing about him.

I almost called Riley, but each version of the conversation I imagined promised to be awkward and not reflective of how I was feeling. For the first time in my life, I felt like an outsider in my own family and—although I was trying not to be—a little resentful of how much had changed in the short time I'd been gone.

I hoped all of that would fall away as soon as I saw that my family was happy. If my mother and sister had found men who were good to them, I would welcome them into the family. Even if they were rich. Even if their presence meant I couldn't step back into the life I'd had before because it was no longer there.

It was late when the ferry docked on the Vineyard. Transportation was readily available, so I grabbed a taxi and gave the driver the address of Dominic's beachside resort. The driver turned in his seat and gave me a once-over. "The old Battencourt place. You starting a job there?" he asked.

Was it the faded jeans? My well-worn sweatshirt? I'd packed some slacks and a button-down shirt in my backpack, but casual was my travel attire. "No, I'm attending an event."

"Lucky you." The man turned forward again and started driving. As he went, he said, "Have you been there before?"

"No. First time on the Vineyard." I sat back and looked out the window. Although I'd grown up within a few hours of the island, my family hadn't made a trip over. Money for such a luxury had simply never been there.

"Too bad, I'd love to hear what's been done to the inside. The place has been around as long as anyone can remember. It was a private residence, part of a naval base at one time, for a while it was a hotel. A popular one too. Then the Corisis bought it, and no one goes in there now. I have a friend who works there every summer and he had to sign an NDA. I asked him what the hell goes on in there that he can't talk about and guess what . . ."

"He won't talk about it?"

"Exactly. He keeps going back, though, so I guess it's not that bad. And he drives a nice car now. So, who am I to judge, right?"

"I guess." It was all so alien to me I couldn't imagine it

ever sounding normal, but I'd have to adapt. If Riley married a wealthy man, this was her world now and I couldn't let that stop us from remaining close. I had a difficult time picturing my mother happy outside of her kitchen, but maybe that was the child in me. I needed more for myself. If she needed more as well, I'd support her.

"These walls?" the driver said as we drove by ten-foot-tall stone walls that lined one side of the road. "The Corisis put them up. Like some medieval fortress. No one on the island would be surprised if they added a moat and parapets. Be glad you didn't fly in today. The airport is a nightmare. World leaders and movie stars don't disrupt the island as much as when the Corisis come or go. The running joke is that they 'occupy' the island rather than visit it. When they leave there is a collective sigh of relief and life goes back to normal."

"I wonder if they have any idea." Like a boat dragging an anchor, Dominic might be completely unaware of how his presence affected the environment around him.

"Oh, shit, I wasn't thinking that you might say something to them. I talk too much. Forget I said anything."

"No worries. Trust me, what you think of the Corisis is the least of my concerns this weekend."

"Thanks." After a moment, he said, "They're not all bad. Get this, there are small businesses on the island that had their mortgages or loans forgiven mysteriously. The Vineyard is a magnet for rich people in the summer; nothing like that happened before the Corisis came. One of my cousins worked for them the first summer they were here. She took them on tours and shit. When she went back to college in the fall? Bam, financial aid had come through that covered her full tuition and her old loans were retroactively paid because a clerical error had been found. She used the money to buy the house next to my mother and now runs it as a bed-and-breakfast."

"Interesting," I said absently. Everything the driver was saying fit what those close to Dominic had told me about him. It wasn't all about testing people. Sometimes Dominic simply used money to show he cared. I could see how building a relationship with him was a process.

Had the yacht been a test or a gift? He'd said it was the latter.

How did Riley feel toward him?

Could my mother actually handle being around him?

I'll soon see for myself.

The driver stopped at the security booth in the middle of two double wide metal gates. A man in a suit approached with a clipboard and asked for my ID. When he read it, he smiled. "Mr. Ragsdale, we were starting to worry you wouldn't make it." He touched an earpiece then said, "Mr. Ragsdale has arrived. Would you like me to escort him? You'll do it? I'll tell him." As he returned my ID, the guard said, "Mr. Stone is on his way. If you'd like to step out of your vehicle, he'll drive you the rest of the way."

I paid the driver with a credit card, added a larger tip than normal, grabbed my backpack, and exited the taxi. Before walking away from it, I thanked the driver again and said, "If it's possible, I'll get you in for a tour sometime."

The driver smiled. "I'd like that. Hey, good luck with whatever you're doing."

I nodded. "Thanks." And turned back to the guard. "All set."

He led me to the inside of the gate where Marc was already stepping out of a vehicle. I swung my backpack over my shoulder and said, "Still in the escort business I see."

The guard beside me coughed.

Marc arched an eyebrow, but one corner of his mouth lifted in a partial smile. "Good to see you again, Kal." I chose the front passenger seat when I got into his car. Once we were both inside, he said, "I heard things went well when you and Dominic spoke. I hope this visit ends better than your first."

"I'm sure it will." I didn't mind that he was tossing shade back my way. In fact, I liked him more for it.

As Marc began to drive, he said, "The complex is a series of suites, each equipped with its own staff. You'll be in the east wing. For logistical reasons, your sister and Gavin's room is on the far side of that building, away from the water and grassy area. A carnival will begin to be set up in that area tomorrow morning. It's a surprise for Riley."

"She loves carnival games." As we drove, I was awed by

the sheer size of the resort. Although it was clapboard and gabled in traditional New England style, there were modern touches everywhere and the building seemed to go on forever in both directions. How could something like this belong to one person?

Marc smiled. "Yes, that's how the theme was chosen. Your family is gathered for dinner now. I can take you directly to see them or to your suite first."

I ran a hand over my neck. "I wouldn't mind freshening up before I see them."

"Perfect. You'll find contact information for key people on the desk in your suite. There's a breakfast in the morning followed by the carnival and hopefully a proposal. More information regarding the weekend's itinerary will also be on the packet on your desk."

"Sounds organized."

Marc parked the car. "Does your family know you're coming?"

"I haven't spoken to them yet, so I'm not sure."

He met my gaze and nodded. "I see and hear a lot because it's my job to pay attention. For what it's worth, Dominic was as nervous about meeting your mother as you probably are about coming here."

"I'm not—" I stopped then cleared my throat and said, "If Riley is happy and my mother feels safe, it doesn't really matter how I feel."

He smiled. "Would you believe Dominic said the same

thing to me yesterday before they arrived? You're more alike than I would have guessed was possible." He held up a hand and said, "Hang on, it's my wife."

He lowered his head and rubbed a hand over his temple. "No, I wasn't informed of that. Yes, I remember you saying you had to pick up something for Dominic. Something— you didn't say *someone*." Marc glanced at me then said, "You thought this was a good idea? Now?" After another pause, he said, "I understand. We're parked at the entrance closest to Kal's suite. I planned to bring him in now. Okay. We'll meet you inside."

Marc's mood had changed enough for me to be concerned. "Something wrong?"

He opened his door. As he got out, he said, "I hope not. I don't miss much, but I didn't see this one coming."

That didn't sound good. I scrambled out of my side of the vehicle. "I don't understand. Who is here who shouldn't be? Why are they a problem?"

"Follow me." Shaking his head, Marc motioned for me to follow. When we came to a glass door, he swiped a card to open it. "And I didn't say they're a problem. That's for you to decide."

I followed Marc into the hotel "Me?" Even as I voiced the question, I froze. Before I had visual confirmation, I *knew*. Then she stepped into the hallway in a tight little dress that knocked my breath clear out of me. "Jade," I said in a hoarse voice.

From her styled hair down to her high heels, she was dressed to impress, and it was *hot*. There wasn't an inch of her I didn't know intimately, and not an inch I didn't crave exploring all over again. *Holy hell.*

Her smile was uncertain, and her stride unsteady as she walked toward me waving. "Surprise."

I forced my legs into motion and met her halfway. "What are you doing here?" I groaned inwardly. That wasn't what I should have led with.

"I wanted to be there for you—here for you—I thought you might need—"

I pulled her into my arms and let my kiss say everything I couldn't articulate. It was passionate, unbridled, and full of wonder. When I raised my head, she looked as shaken as I felt. "Thank you."

"You're welcome." Her voice was delightfully breathless. Our eyes remained locked on each other as she raised a hand to caress my cheek. "You're sure it's okay that I'm here?"

"More than okay. It's *right* that you are."

Her happiness shone from her eyes. "That's how the decision to come here felt—right."

I couldn't resist the next kiss I gave her, or the one after that.

In the background I heard Marc say, "Okay, okay, he seems fine with this. Let's get out of here."

Between kisses, I murmured, "I'm so fine with this."

She smiled beneath my kisses. "I'm glad." When I lifted

my head, she said, "We each have our own suite, but if you'd like—"

"I'd like." After pulling her to my chest for a hug, I said, "Lead the way."

"I believe they're identical, both with views of the ocean."

I stepped back and took her hand in mine. "You're the only view I need."

That made her laugh. "Oh, you've been working on your game, huh?"

I caught and held her gaze. "None of this is a game to me, Jade. I'm glad you're here." She went to hug me and tripped. I caught her, steadying her against my side. "I knew you were falling for me, but . . ."

Her cheeks flushed. "Sorry. I've never worn heels this high." She glanced down. "Or a dress this tight."

I looked her up and down. "You look amazing in that, but you were also stunning in shorts and a T-shirt."

She used her free hand to reference her dress. "Alethea—have you met her, by the way?"

"I have."

"She took me shopping on the way here. This dress is supposed to make you forget you didn't actually invite me."

I dropped my backpack and placed my hands on her hips, turning her to face me fully. "It only took one kiss to do that." She was so damn earnest. I'd grown used to people interacting with me on a superficial level. They'd seen my act and wanted a taste of the fantasy. Jade looked deeper and whatever the hell she saw in me . . . I didn't want to ever disappoint her again. "Consider yourself formally invited to join me on whatever adventure life presents."

She brought her hands up, flat on my chest. "You mean that."

I rested my forehead briefly on hers. "I do."

"Kal, I won't be offended if you don't want to introduce me to your family. I just wanted—"

"My mom will want to feed you. My sister will ask you a thousand questions, but she loves everyone so it's not to pass judgement. She just really wants to know." I raised my head. "They'll love you." *Because they'll see all the reasons I do.* I kept that last part to myself.

"I hope so. I know this sounds ridiculous, but I'm nervous. I wasn't when I agreed to come, but when Alethea told me the kind of people who are here . . . I didn't want to embarrass you." She glanced down at her feet. "I should have brought some of my low heels, but I didn't own anything nice enough for this weekend."

I tipped her chin upward, so our gazes met. "Everything you own is good enough or neither of us belong here." I nodded toward my backpack on the floor beside me. "I packed slacks and a button-down shirt. It's an important day for my sister, so I'll wear something nice, but I'd rather wear an ill-fitting wetsuit than a tux."

"That's quite an image," she said with a smile. "Somehow I bet you'd look good in both."

I wiggled my eyebrows at her. "Why don't we go change you into something more comfortable."

"I'm all for that," she said with a sexy smile. "But just so you know, all I have with me is more of this. I'm grateful to Alethea. She was so excited to dress me I didn't know how to tell her none of it was my style."

I could see how a pleaser like Jade would be swayed by Alethea's enthusiasm and confidence. I picked up my backpack. "Let's go to my room for a minute."

"Just a minute? That's fast," she said cheekily, and I sucked in a breath as we exchanged a heated look. It would have been easy to carry her into either of our rooms and forget about everything else. My body was clamoring to get her alone, but my heart wanted her to meet my family as herself, not uncomfortable and dressed by someone else. The problem was I was still cash poor. If I combined a few of my bank accounts . . .

A man interrupted my thoughts by saying, "Excuse me, Mr. Ragsdale?"

I reluctantly turned to greet him. "Yes."

The man was tall, proud, immaculately dressed, and probably ten years older than I was. "My name is Paul. I'll be your butler for the weekend. Is there any luggage you'd like me to take in?"

Distracted, I handed him my backpack, then had to hold back a smile when he took it like one would accept a bag of rattlesnakes. "I'll put it in your room," he said.

I made the mistake of checking Jade's expression. As soon as Paul turned to walk to my room, she made a face. I shrugged. *Don't laugh. Do not laugh.*

We followed Paul to my room where I thanked him and gave him a five-dollar bill. I would have tipped bigger, but it was all I had in my wallet. He blinked a few times, then pocketed the bill. "If there is anything you need, sir, anything at all, my number is on the outside of the packet on your desk. I'm on call for the weekend, so the hour is irrelevant."

Anything, huh? I let go of Jade's hand and said, "I do have a question for you." I shot a quick look at Jade. "Do you mind if I ask him something alone?"

"Alone?" Her mouth rounded. "Oh. Sure. My suite is the next door down on the right."

"It'll just take a minute."

Jade looked confused, but not upset. "Okay. Take your time." She teetered her way out the door into the hallway.

As soon as she was out, I closed the door. "Paul, it's pretty obvious I don't fit in here."

Paul's only response was a raising and lowering of his eyebrows.

"I don't care what people think of me." I glanced back at the door. "But see that woman? She means the world to me, and I want her to feel confident when she meets my family. Alethea meant well, but Jade has a simpler style. Do you know of any stores on the island where a person with limited, really limited, funds could find something suitable but not as . . . nightclub-ish?"

He gave me a long look. He gave me another once-over. Rather than make him voice the questions I saw in his eyes, I said, "Riley Ragsdale is my sister but that doesn't mean I could afford this trip." He didn't appear to believe me, so I took out my phone and brought up photos of my mother's apartment in Lockton. "This was my life until recently. That's my mother, she makes amazing sauce but rock-hard meatballs." I swiped to another photo. "That's Riley and me sitting out on the fire escape like it was a balcony. I grew up to the sound of gunshots in the background to the point where it was normal to us." I put my phone away and said, "All I'm trying to do is survive here, not embarrass my family, and make this a good experience for the woman I love . . ." I glanced back at the door again. Although I hadn't told Jade yet how I felt, I'd never been more certain about anything. Her leap of faith in coming to the Vineyard to support me had erased any lingering doubts. It was no longer a matter of if we'd be together or if she'd take me back. *She's here.*

It's my turn to step up to the plate.

Paul remained silent.

I shook my head. "I know. None of this is your problem. And the crappy tip? It was all I had on me. Give me your info and I'll send you something when I get home. I won't be broke for long. I'm not just dreaming anymore—I'm taking action."

He cocked his head to one side and pursed his lips before asking, "What kind of action?"

It didn't take much to get me talking about what I was enthusiastic about. I told him about how the dive in Catalina had opened my eyes to the issues with anchors. I went off on a tangent about how while working a job I hated I kept my sanity by reading up on marine biologists and reaching out to them whenever I could. "My goal now is to parlay those connections into a project that would have a meaningful impact on the ocean floor as well as pay the bills." I crossed my fingers in the air. "I'm waiting for a callback from someone at Netflix. It's a wild shot. If I don't hear from them, I'm not giving up. This project *will* happen."

He frowned then his whole demeanor changed. "You're not at all who I expected you to be."

I was genuinely curious. "In a good way?"

"Absolutely." He nodded toward the window. "My sister owns a boutique on the island. She'd probably have something your friend would like."

"Really? Thanks. If you give me the address . . ."

"It would be closed this late in the day."

"Yeah."

"And most of the clothing is expensive."

"Well, it was an idea, anyway." I sighed. "I'll figure something out."

He took out his phone and sent a text. A moment later he repocketed his phone and said, "Marilyn said she would love to comp your girlfriend a dress. She believes she might also have a suit that would fit you."

"Oh, I don't need—"

"You will tomorrow. It would be at no cost as well." He pinned me with a look. "Just mention Marilyn's boutique and she'll be happy."

"Of course." I remembered the low quality of the trousers and shirt I'd brought. The only suits or tuxes I owned had clasps that allowed for one pull removals, and I'd left them at the last club I'd worked. "I'll make sure she benefits from this."

"I believe you." He added, "She agreed to meet you at her boutique now if that works for you."

"Works for me? Are you kidding? This is amazing!" I went to give his arm a slug but held back and composed myself. "If you give me the address, I'll call for a car."

"It's suggested that all guests use the drivers who were brought in for the event. I'll arrange a car to meet you outside the door closest to your room." He motioned to the direction Marc and I had entered through.

"Thank you, Paul."

"You're welcome, Mr. Ragsdale. It's my pleasure to ensure that your time here is enjoyable."

I had to ask. "Is it? Do you like what you do?"

His face relaxed and for the first time his smile reached

his eyes. "I do. It's interesting, and I'm not a butler full time. I have a small bistro on the Vineyard. My grandmother was French and when people enjoy her old recipes . . . she smiles down on me." He cleared his throat. "One of the guests this weekend is Chef Richard D'Argenson. His restaurants are top notch; all have three Michelin stars which is practically unheard of. To be so close to someone I have such admiration for . . . how could I not love being here?"

"Have you had a chance to meet him?"

"Oh, no," Paul said with a proud rise of his chin. "We're not allowed to interact with guests beyond the ones assigned to us."

That was a shame. "What would you say to him if you had the chance to talk to him?"

"Nothing." Paul's smile returned. "I'd serve him my grandmother's bouillabaisse. No words would be necessary. I'd see his reaction and so would she." He stopped and adjusted his suit jacket. "We all have dreams, don't we? That's mine. Now, if you don't require anything else, I'll arrange the transportation for you and Miss Tremblay."

"Thank you, Paul." As I made my way to Jade's room, an idea came to me for how I could repay Paul for his kindness. The side mission would not only be a welcome distraction, but I had the feeling it was one Jade would enjoy helping me with.

I knocked on her door. When she opened it with a huge smile, still rocking that tight little dress and high heels, I asked, "Ready to go shopping? Let's get you into something that suits you."

Her smile faded.

Shit. That came out wrong. I added hastily, "Not that you look bad like that."

Her eyebrows arched.

I rolled my shoulders back and swallowed hard. "I found a boutique that's reopening just for us. A car is coming to take us there now."

"For a *second* makeover today?" She folded her arms across her chest. I tried not to focus on how delightfully that move rounded her breasts above the neckline of her dress.

I'm sure I looked like a deer caught in headlights. "I thought—" I cleared my throat. "You seemed to want—Oh, hell, just close the door and let me start over."

When she closed the door in my face, I wasn't entirely certain it would reopen when I knocked on it again. It did. Her smile wasn't as bright, but her arms were at her sides again. "Hello."

I started by leaning forward and kissing her sweet lips, slowly, gently. The warm way she returned that kiss went a long way to reassure me that my gaff was forgiven. When I raised my head I said, "I found a place where I can get a suit for tomorrow. Would you like to come shopping with me?"

Her smile widened. "I would love to." She linked her arm in mine. "Hopefully they have lower heeled shoes."

I closed the door to her room behind us. "Who knows?

You might find something you like as well."

She glanced up at me and gave my arm a shake. "I felt really sexy standing in that doorway."

I stopped and turned her to me. "Hold on. Do you think it's easy to not haul you off to the nearest bed? My mind is racing with all the things I want to do with you, to you, watch you do to me. But—" I tucked a loose hair back into her updo. I almost said the words, but they just didn't come out yet. "You matter to me. How you feel matters. I thought earlier you were saying you weren't comfortable in the clothes you'd brought. If I was wrong . . ."

She swayed toward me. "You weren't." Then she blushed. "I'm sorry. I probably had too much time to think about it. I actually practiced which pose . . . Oh, God, I feel ridiculous."

"Jade." If I hadn't known that Paul's sister was waiting for us, I would have shown her how good I'd found it. Instead, I gave her forehead a kiss and growled, "Don't doubt yourself—or us. Just because we're still figuring each other out, doesn't mean I'm not all in."

She searched my face then said, "I'm all in too, and it's fucking scary."

I laughed and tucked her under my chin. "We've got this."

When I released her, she laced her hand with mine and asked, "Finding a store was what you talked to Paul about?"

"Yes." As we walked out of the building, I remembered

an earlier thought and my voice rose with excitement. "And I came up with a challenge for you and me."

"A challenge?"

"We are going to find a way to get one Richard D'Argenson to eat at my butler's restaurant."

She chuckled. "What are you talking about?"

For her to understand, I would need to come clean about why I'd asked Paul for help. I thought back to my stage persona. Women loved a confident alpha male. I'd made a career out of putting my anger on display.

I didn't feel angry when I was with Jade.

She'd told me she didn't care that I was starting over. She'd done nothing to imply she judged me for my current state of finances, but there was a difference between knowing and living the experience with me.

I waited until we were in the car before I started to tell her what Paul and I had discussed. Her hand tightened on mine a few times, but she listened without interrupting.

CHAPTER TWENTY-ONE

Jade

A S I LISTENED to Kal share why he'd asked for a few minutes alone with Paul and what they'd talked about, I was struck by the beauty of what he'd done. This proud man had humbled himself for *me*—because he wanted to take care of me.

He'd done the same for his family when he'd taken the stage to raise money for his mother's medical bills. It couldn't have been easy to tell me he couldn't afford to take me on a shopping spree. So many men would have closed me out, but Kal didn't. He wanted to be real with me more than he wanted to impress me. That was a man I could imagine spending a lifetime with.

Dominic had said: *If he's not good enough for you when he's down, then you're not good enough for him when he rises.* I was tempted to tell Kal that I didn't care about his financial situation, but it was clear that it mattered to him. I understood that because my grandfather was proud that way.

Kal wasn't soft the way many modern men were. He stepped up, stepped in when he saw someone in need. I wondered if having his mother rely on him from such a young age had made him stronger, more empathetic, and more traditional in values despite his stage career.

"Kal, I love all of this," I said in a gush.

He looked surprised.

"I love your honesty, your heart, the way you care about everyone. I see good things coming your way this year."

He leaned closer to my ear and growled, "How about tonight?"

I laughed and turned so I could look him in the eye. "Absolutely." We kissed briefly and my heart soared. This was how love was supposed to feel. Light. Happy. Free. "So, we have *two* goals for this weekend."

"Only two?" he murmured, and I flushed because I knew exactly where his thoughts had wandered.

I slapped his thigh. "Besides that. One, D'Argenson needs to taste Paul's grandmother's recipe and two, we need to look so good in Marilyn's clothing that your brother's rich friends will flock to her boutique."

His smile warmed me to my toes. "I'm up for both."

A quick glance downward confirmed that he was indeed up. I ran a hand suggestively up his thigh. "I'm glad you find this conversation so—exciting."

He chuckled and let out a slow breath. "I'll let you in on a secret . . . all you have to do to have this effect on me is show up. No, that's not true. Just the thought of you is also potent torture."

As I was about to respond, the driver announced we'd arrived at the boutique. I shimmied out, and while focusing on keeping my dress from hiking up too far, caught one of my heels on the edge of the sidewalk and stumbled. *Damn these shoes and this stupid dress.*

I glanced back and saw far too much amusement in Kal's eyes. "You think you could walk in these?"

"No, ma'am."

I wagged a playful finger in his direction. "Then keep those thoughts to yourself."

Sporting a huge grin, he brought a hand to his chest. "I didn't say anything."

It was impossible to not smile back, but I waved in the general direction of his face. "But everything you're thinking is right there in your eyes."

His expression turned more serious, and his voice lowered. "Is it?"

Our gaze locked and for a moment I forgot where we were. There was nothing beyond him and the raw emotion I saw in his eyes—no—yes? Afraid to believe that this could happen so fast, I looked away.

He put his hand on my lower back to usher me toward the entrance of the boutique. I held my breath and waited for him to say something, but before he did the door of the shop opened.

The woman who greeted us was tall and thin, perhaps a few years older than we were, and in a navy linen dress. Her hair was pulled back in a timeless, relaxed fashion that fit the island. "Welcome. Come on in. I'm Marilyn." She referenced the sign above the shop's all-white front. *Marilyn's Closet.*

The mannequins on either side of the door were dressed in casual nautical attire. As if she'd read my mind, she said, "I also have formalwear. It's in the back. I sell a lot of original pieces my mother and I design."

My heart warmed at the idea of a family run shop. "Thank you so much for opening for us," I said as I stepped through the glass door she held open. The inside was bright, but modestly decorated. Clothing was hung from rods on both sides at various heights and a white painted table displayed folded shirts and slacks.

"You look familiar," she said to Kal.

"I have one of those faces," Kal answered without missing a beat.

I glanced back, wondering if she recognized Kal from the stage or a poster. It was easy to forget that he was also Invio. Her expression gave nothing away.

Once inside, she took the lead. "We'll head to the back." As we walked, she took another look at Kal. "I'm pretty good with faces. I feel like I should know you. Should I? Are you on the big screen?"

Kal shook his head. "My name is Kal Ragsdale." He put his arm around my waist and introduced me. "This is my girlfriend, Jade Tremblay."

"Doesn't ring a bell." She tapped her temple. "It'll come to me. It always does."

"I do look a lot like my brother, Dominic Corisi. That could be it."

Surprised that he'd shared that, I gave Kal a quick look. Oh, I get it, he was looking to distract her.

Marilyn didn't appear impressed by the name drop. "I do see the resemblance, but that's not it. Sorry. It'll come to me when I no longer care for it to." She gave Kal a head-to-toe look and said, "I don't have a suit on the floor that would fit a man of your . . . size. However, I do have some clients I always keep something on hand for. Do you mind if I take your measurements?"

"Not at all," Kal said.

I would have said the same until Marilyn took her time with that measuring tape. She fumbled, dropped it, had to measure several parts of his body more than once. The pink flush to her face was her biggest giveaway.

I was feeling a little territorial until I noticed he didn't seem affected by her at all. He made a few jokes, but none that were flirtatious.

From beside them I asked, "Will you need my measurements as well?"

Without looking away from Kal, Marilyn said, "I'm sure I have something off the rack that will fit you."

My mouth dropped open, my eyes widened, and I could have sworn that Kal coughed back a laugh. When Marilyn stepped away to check what she had in the back, I slapped Kal's arm.

He chuckled and shot me a boyishly guilty smile. "I can't help it if women find me irresistible. If you want, we'll find a shop tomorrow that's run by a man and he can . . . hold on, no. I don't like that idea at all."

"Exactly."

He squared his shoulders. "Don't worry. I've got your back." When Marilyn returned, Kal said, "Jade flew up to meet my family. Tomorrow is about my sister getting engaged, but it won't be long before Jade and I head down that same road. Don't tell Jade, but I'm already hers."

I blinked a few times quickly. He was either an incredibly good actor, or that was how he felt. *Oh, my God.*

"That is so sweet." She turned to me. "Is this really the first time you're meeting his family?"

I clasped my hands in front of me and took a page out of Kal's book. Maybe if she knew me a little better she'd be less quick to dismiss me. I motioned toward my skintight dress. "A friend gave me a makeover today, but this isn't how I usually dress. I can't walk in these heels. I'm surprised I haven't already broken an ankle."

Marilyn's eyebrows drew together. "What is your normal style?"

"I'm a marine biologist. Not a lot of dresses in my closet."

Her expression softened. "My uncle went to school for

that. He has a desk job in insurance now, but he's always loved the ocean." She looked me over again. "Tell me about tomorrow's event."

Kal jumped in with the basics—a breakfast and a beach-side carnival.

"I have a few pieces that might work."

When she approached me with the measuring tape, I beamed a smile at Kal and wiggled my eyebrows. *I won her over.*

He nodded and winked.

"Yes," she said. "It should fit. I have an elderly client who loves garden dresses. Simple, classic styles. I'll bring out a few for you to try on. She always says she likes clothes she can wear to church or to meet the Queen. I think you'll be pleased." To Kal she added, "Jason Momoa was here already this season. He doesn't normally return so I doubt he'll miss any of the suits I put aside for him. If you find one you like, I'm not even sure I'll have to tailor it."

Of course.

I get the granny dress.

He gets Aquaman's suit.

"I'll be right back with a few outfits for each of you to try on."

"Thank you," I said politely even though I was inwardly rolling my eyes.

When Marilyn was out of the room, Kal flexed. "I'll help you across the street later if you need assistance, Granny."

"You're an ass," I said, but I was smiling.

He kissed me and murmured, "You know, there isn't a dress she could bring out here that you wouldn't look gorgeous in."

Bring on the granny dress, Marilyn.

I need to get this man alone.

CHAPTER TWENTY-TWO

Kal

LIKE MOST MEN, I don't normally like to shop, especially for clothing, but anything I did with Jade was fun. Her expression when Marilyn had said she'd bring out dresses she'd made for an elderly client—priceless. I doubt a saint could have resisted teasing her about that one.

With Marilyn out of the room, I could focus all of my attention on Jade and how damn good it felt to be with her. I lightly kissed her sweet lips again, savoring how something as innocent as that could set my entire body on fire. The way she smiled between kisses sent my heart racing. I should have been in a rush to get her alone, but it had been a long time— too long—since I'd simply enjoyed someone's company and there was nothing about being with Jade that I wanted to rush.

"How do you not have an enormous ego?" she asked.

I loved that she knew I didn't put much stock into the superficial. "I didn't get into lifting weights to impress anyone. I was twelve when my mother's back started to spasm so badly she couldn't walk for a while. I was nowhere near this size and the first time I tried to pick her up, I dropped her."

Jade's eyes rounded and her expression filled with sympathy. "Oh, that's awful. You couldn't get a nurse to come in?"

"My mother was afraid of strangers. I understand why now, but back then Riley and I accepted it as normal. We took care of her the best we could."

She ran a hand through the hair on my temple. "You had to grow up so fast, didn't you?"

"I guess. I don't have another childhood to compare it to. But it made me strong, in more ways than one." Memories of the neighborhood gym I'd practically grown up in came back to me then and a smile lifted a corner of my mouth.

She nodded. "I sense there's a story in there. What are you thinking?"

"About the first time I met Sal. I was angry with myself after dropping my mother. She was a small woman, but I hadn't had a major growth spurt yet. Anyway, I'd seen him around the neighborhood and asked him what the secret was to getting stronger."

"And what did he say?"

"He laughed. I was scrawny. He probably thought I wanted to build up to look better, but then I told him why I needed to be strong."

Jade's eyes shone with emotion. "So you could help move your mother from room to room?"

"That's what I told him. Riley could help her shower, but she couldn't lift her."

"And?"

"And Sal invited me to his gym and let me train for free. There I was, this little runt, whose voice hadn't even changed yet, learning strength training with body-building competitors. Straight through middle and high school I was there before and after school either working out or helping clean the gym. Those men became my second family." I smiled as good memories came flooding back. "They built people up from the inside out. I can still hear Sal saying: Anyone who has the time or desire to try to bring you down is already below you."

"That's so true. Are you still close?"

I looked away before answering. "We stayed in touch when I was in college, but then I started dancing. It's a different lifestyle and I got swept into the wild side of it for a while. Lots of partying. Lots of substance abuse. Nothing I want to go back to, but I became someone they didn't recognize or like."

"Have you considered going back?"

I had, but I'd never been able to bring myself to do it. "They lost respect for me." It was the first time I'd said it aloud or allowed myself to face that harsh truth.

"Then they're missing out on an amazing man." She laid a hand flat on my chest. "Remember when I said I wouldn't bring Invio home? That's not true anymore. I've gotten to know him. He paid for your mother's first surgery, nearly paid for her second one as well. There is nothing he wouldn't do for his family, and even when he's angry—it's kind of hot."

I smiled at that. "Really? Hold on, so you liked my show?"

She fluttered her lashes and peered through them up at me. "Well, I *am* human."

"We may have to compare acts sometime." I wrapped my arms around her waist and hugged her.

Her face went bright red. "Oh, I couldn't."

Adorable, but not true. With a grin, I challenged, "You could for me."

Her chest rose and fell against mine. "As long as you don't laugh."

"Trust me, that's the last thing I'd do." Then I winked. "Unless your little show starts with you in a granny dress, then I might chuckle a little."

"Granny dress." She made a face at me. "Now I'm determined to leave here with something nice." She glanced down. "A little less like I'm for hire for the night, but enough to knock your socks off."

Against her forehead I murmured, "Do you really not see how you don't even have to try to do that?"

She melted into my embrace, and we stood there for a moment, breathing each other in.

Too soon, Marilyn returned with a selection for each of

us to try on. I asked her to give us a few minutes alone to decide. She agreed and headed off to another part of the shop. There were two changing rooms so we each headed into one. I quickly shed my clothing, not wanting to miss a single one of the dresses she might model for me.

The first suit was a little too flashy for me, but I put it on anyway and headed out to show Jade. She stepped out of her room in an ankle-length yellow floral dress. The sleeves were poofed and it reminded me of a Victorian woman, but the neckline dipped low, making it also a winner in my book. "You look gorgeous in that one," I said.

"You look," she bit her lip then wrinkled her nose. "Shiny?"

I nodded. "That's what I thought. I'll go try on the next."

"Me too."

The next suit I chose was steel gray and more traditional. I felt like I was ready to apply for a job at a bank. I exited just as Jade did. This time she was in a sleeveless knee-length flowered dress that reminded me of rose quartz. The pattern was simple and flowing. The color made her cheeks glow. "You also look incredible in that."

She looked me over. "That one is nice. Are you comfortable in it?"

I flexed my shoulders. "It fits, but not really."

She nodded. "I have one last one."

"Same."

With a smile we both turned and reentered our changing rooms. The last suit was the more casual of the three, dark blue with a modern cut. Marilyn had paired it with a black cotton tee rather than a dress shirt. I liked it because I could shed the jacket and be comfortable, but still presentable.

Jade was already outside, waiting for me. As soon as she saw me, she said, "That's the one."

I smiled. "That's what I thought." Now her dress on the other hand looked as if it had been made from vintage curtains. "That's—that's—a lot of really big flowers."

"Really? But this was my favorite." She looked so disappointed I instantly felt bad.

I did a hasty rewind. "But it suits you."

She burst out laughing. "Now I know you're full of shit because this one is horrid."

I laughed along with her, more than a little relieved. "It does look like it was made for someone three times your age."

With a huge smile Jade spun before me. "You said I could rock any dress."

"I did and you do. Looks like that's your dress."

When she stopped spinning, she steadied herself with a hand on my shoulder. "Only if you wear the shiny suit."

I chuckled. "What a pair we would be."

She ran her hand down the front lapel of my jacket. "I do like this one, though." Then she tilted her head to the side and said, "Of the other two, which dress did you prefer?"

I laid my hand over hers and searched her face. "Which one did you feel the most beautiful in?"

"The pink one."

I bent and kissed her briefly. "Then that's my favorite."

"Let's tell Marilyn and get out of here."

She didn't have to say that twice. We changed quickly, thanked Marilyn with the same level of urgency, and texted the car to return for us. I kept my hands off her on the ride back out of respect. Hand in hand we carried our packaged clothing down the hall to my suite, but as soon as we were inside, we tossed the outfits over the back of a chair, and I swung her over my shoulder.

"Hey," she said between laughs. "What is this?"

I strode to the bedroom and tossed her on my king-size bed. "Tonight, you fuck Invio."

She scrambled to sit up. Her eyes were wide, but there was a fire burning in them that told me she'd enjoy the roleplay as much as I would. She flicked her tongue across her bottom lip. "Okay."

There were still old playlists on my phone. I started one, turned the volume way up, and set my phone aside. The music pulsed through the room as I held her gaze and channeled the energy that had carried me through my shows. I had to dig deep because I wasn't angry anymore, but the body remembers and when I tore my shirt over my head, I did it with all the power and attitude I was known for.

She gasped.

I kicked off my shoes and socks but kept my jeans on. Returning to the stage in my mind I claimed the space before the bed, ran my hand over my chest and down the front of my stomach to the belt of my jeans, over my cock, and thrust forward against my hand.

I leaned in close to her, but not so close that she could touch me, then did a body roll. I stepped closer, spread my legs a little wider, and did another, this time running my hands down my thighs as I thrust them forward.

I switched to a fan favorite, fists together in front of my chest while I rotated my hips in slow circles to the rhythm of the music. Jade hadn't moved.

I reached out, pulled her forward to the edge of the bed, and said, "I dance better for a naked audience."

When she kicked off her shoes, I started dancing again. When she paused before removing her dress, I paused as well. My moves were her reward and she understood quickly.

The imp took her time with each article of clothing, prolonging the dance, controlling it by stopping and starting her own strip. Naked she reached for me, but I growled, "No one touches Invio."

Her hands dropped away, and her mouth parted.

"Sit on the bed."

She sat.

I kept my moves smooth and in sync with the throbbing beat of the music. I turned, rolled my hips, and undid my jeans, kicking them off to the side. I bent forward, boxer briefs tented over my excitement, as I arched my shoulders and rolled my ass within touching distance.

I turned, took a moment to appreciate the perfection of her bare tits, and placed a foot on the bed beside her, keeping my body moving. I claimed her space, fucked her without touching her, and kept my expression angry as I did so.

She was flushed from head to toe, her eyes burning with hunger for what I wouldn't give her. I picked up one of her hands, brought it to my lips, and sucked her middle finger into my mouth. I circled it as I'd have her circle me later, then brought her hand to her own sex and said, "Make yourself come for me, Jade. Watch me. Imagine me on you, inside you, taking what I want. Give me everything while I give you nothing."

"This is nothing?" she asked hoarsely.

I pushed her finger between her folds and bent over her. "Do it, Jade."

She closed her eyes and started moving her hand back and forth over herself. I grabbed her chin and growled, "With your eyes open. I want your eyes on me."

We were so close her breath was a hot caress on my lips. I didn't kiss her though. Invio wouldn't have and this was her fantasy.

She started off by only fingering herself, but as she got more excited, she became more creative. Her free hand came up to cup her own breast then pinch her nipple.

While she brought herself pleasure, I returned to dancing for her, but our eyes remained locked. I dove to the floor, then hopped back to my feet and stripped my remaining clothing off.

With my cock freed, I continued to move close and away, so close her breathing would change and then away before she could touch me. She was visibly wet and closing in on an orgasm when I placed a foot beside her on the bed and fisted my hand in the hair on the back of her neck. She opened her mouth for me. I dragged her forward and around my cock. Her lips closed around me eagerly. "Don't stop pleasing yourself, Jade. I want my cock in your mouth when you come."

She shifted her position, so she spread her legs wider. The things that woman did with her tongue and lips were sinful and so fucking good. She moved her head back and forth, accepting me deeper and deeper until I thought I'd orgasm before she did.

When she came, she made a delightful sound that vibrated over my cock. She tensed then shuddered and relaxed. I withdrew from her mouth and told her to turn so she was on her knees facing away from me. I took hold of her hair again and held her in position while I ran my cock back and forth over her wet sex.

There was no gentleness in me, and I doubted she wanted any. I hauled her back and thrust my cock deep. Her cry of, "Oh, God, yes," was all I needed to take it to the next level.

There's sex and then there is fucking. Fucking doesn't ask permission. It's rough and greedy. It's when a man puts all civility aside and takes a woman.

I pounded into Jade then turned her over and fucked her from above. She clung to me, called out my name, even cried a little. I kept taking, kept thrusting deeper and deeper, harder and harder. She was mine for the taking and I took her until I couldn't hold back any longer and spilled into her. She jutted around me as she had her own orgasm.

Spent, I withdrew from her and rolled onto my side, pulling her into my arms as I did. I kissed her deeply then tucked one of her sweaty curls to the side of her face and said, "So that's Invio."

She swallowed visibly then kissed my chest. "Wow."

I let out a relaxed chuckle. "So, you like it rough, do you?"

She snuggled closer. "I like you. Gentle. Rough. All of you."

"Jade, I—"

She put a hand over my mouth and said, "I don't want to talk." Mimicking the body roll I'd done earlier, she moved against me in a wave. "I think I could come again."

I'd been about to tell her I loved her, but it could wait. I joked, "Again? I don't know if Invio does that."

"Kal does," she murmured and brought one of her hands

to her sex. "He does the most amazing thing with his tongue."

How could any man refuse a woman that?

I certainly couldn't.

I kissed my way across her chest and down her stomach. She spread her legs for me, and I took her to heaven for a third time that night and loved every moment of it.

CHAPTER TWENTY-THREE

Jade

I WOKE IN the middle of the night to the wonder of Kal's arms wrapped around me, his body warming the back of mine. I turned so I could see his face in the dim lighting from a lamp we'd forgotten was on.

I love this man.

He's officially ruined me for all other men. My Kal. My Invio.

Why doesn't he see what a beautiful soul he has?

His eyes fluttered open, and he groaned, "I'm sleeping."

I smiled. "Then who is talking?"

He closed his eyes again. "No one. We're all sleeping."

I snuggled closer then glanced around for a clock so I could check the time. Today would be a big day for him. I prayed it would be everything he needed it to be. His family had suffered enough—he had as well. My heart had broken for him when he'd talked about the men at the gym back home. He'd been hurting when he'd pulled away from them. Just as he'd been hurting when he'd pulled away from his family. And me.

I thought about the little boy who had walked off into the neighborhood in search of a strong man who could help him and realized he'd gone in search of what my grandfather had given me—a father figure. Strength wasn't something he'd found in his home, so he'd needed to look for it elsewhere.

I raised my head. "Kal, I just figured you out."

Without opening his eyes, he said, "Thank God. I was worried it might take you until morning."

I snuggled to his chest again and smiled. "You're grumpy."

"No, I'm sleeping. The telltale difference? My eyes are closed."

A thought came to me, and I voiced it before I had a chance to filter it. "Did you tell your mother and sister that you'd be here?"

"No."

I ran my hand across his muscled chest. "I think I understand why you wouldn't."

He rolled onto his back but kept an arm around my waist. "You want to tell me now, don't you?"

I closed my eyes dutifully. "It can wait."

He pulled me closer and kissed my forehead. "Just say it."

I looked him in the eye and shared what my heart told me I needed to say. "You pull away because you've had to find your strength outside of your family. And you think that being strong is what your family always needs you to be."

He held my gaze without speaking.

I continued, "It's okay to not have the answers, Kal. It's okay to be confused, angry, or sad sometimes. Life can knock us to our knees. I have to believe that families are healthier when they stay and share that with each other. I'm stronger than I look. You need someone to lean on now and then? Lean on me. If you stumble, I'll help you haul your ass right back to your feet. We can be that for each other. We'll share the good and the bad. Just don't pull away from me when things get tough. I've been left behind before and that's my—"

He kissed me then. "Jade, how do you see me clearer than I see myself?"

I traced the strong line of his jaw. "I mean it, Kal. Today might be confusing for you. Don't close me out of that. Let me be part of your strength just like you've been part of mine. You pushed me to take a second look at what I was accepting from others and expecting from myself." I gave his chest a pat. "I could never have been an astronaut's wife. I'm not happy sitting back and waiting for someone to return to me. I want to go on the adventure too . . . even when the going is rough."

He sighed. "There's something I should tell you."

I tensed then forced myself to relax. I either trusted Kal or I didn't. "What is it?"

"When Dominic and I spoke the last time, he gave me some advice on how I could turn my connections with known marine biologists into a profitable project. I've been working on it. Bilboa spoke to his contact at Netflix, and he believes they'll call me. So far, though, it's just a lead. It may not pan out. After this weekend I'll also follow up on other leads. I'll have to find a job to tide me over until something comes through." He cleared his throat. "I'm realistic about the possibility that Netflix might not call."

I searched his face. "Do you think that makes you less amazing? Kal Ragsdale, if you think I'm with you in the hope you're going to be famous one day, you get your ass out of my bed right now."

He smiled. "Technically it's my bed. Your room is next door."

I smacked his chest. "You know what I mean."

"I do." He followed that with another quick kiss then gave me a long look. "There's another reason I haven't spoken to my family yet."

I held my breath and waited.

He added, "I was so angry before I met you, angry to my core. I'd given up feeling any other way. When I'm with you I feel—free of that. I don't want to go back, but I don't know how I'll react if my mother doesn't feel safe here. What if Riley's fiancé is a douche? I keep hearing how good everything is now, but what if it's not and that's what I see tomorrow? I'd do anything for them, but I finally have something to lose, and I don't want to do anything that will mess up what you and I have."

"I love you." There, I'd said it.

His arms tightened around me. "I love you too."

We lay there for a while simply breathing the moment in. Then I said, "Kal, I don't have all the answers, but I did learn something from Robert. I learned that love shouldn't cost someone their soul. It's not healthy to give more than you receive or bend so much that you're a pretzel version of yourself. Good love, real love, doesn't demand that. Your family doesn't want you to give up everything for them. I wouldn't want you to do that for me. Who are you, Kal? Who do you want to be? Be strong, be proud, but don't give so much to anyone that you stop being you."

He breathed in deeply. "I fucking love you."

I laughed, my heart soaring. "We've established that."

"I wish we'd met after this—once I had all my shit together."

"I wasn't proud of who I was when you met me. But maybe we were supposed to start here. We're on a journey to somewhere better . . . not alone . . . together."

His next kiss was so sweet, so tender it led to the kind of lovemaking that was every bit as wonderful as the night before, but entirely different. It was full of whispers and promises, and if there was a single corner of my heart that wasn't already his—I gave it to him that night.

CHAPTER TWENTY-FOUR

Kal

A LOUD KNOCK on the outer door of my suite woke me. Half-asleep I reluctantly left Jade in the bed, pulled on my jeans, and went to answer it.

Paul gave me a once-over then waved his hands in agitation. "I don't want to intrude, but I've been texting and calling you."

I looked around. Rubbing my hand over my face, I said, "Shit, I think I left my phone at your sister's boutique."

"I'll have her bring it over. Right now, you need to hurry. Your family is finishing breakfast. They're headed from there out to the carnival area where the proposal is expected to happen right away. If you don't get your ass in gear, you're going to miss it."

His tone had my eyebrows rising, but he was right. "How much time do you think we have?"

"Ten minutes to get ready. Five minutes of sprinting there. I'll be outside the door waiting for you. If you get dressed fast, I'll make sure you're there in time."

"On it." I closed the door and bolted to the bedroom.

"Jade. Get up. We're late. I'm about to take the world's shortest shower. We have ten minutes to get ready. Can you do it?"

She sat straight up. "I'll make it happen."

We rushed around each other, taking turns showering, brushing our teeth side by side then throwing on clothing. Her hair was up in a loose bun, her face fresh from a wash but bare of makeup as she hastily slipped on the low heel sandals we'd gotten from Marilyn.

Beating the deadline by almost two minutes we paused at the door. She straightened the neckline of my shirt. I tucked the edge of her bra beneath the material of her dress. "Ready?"

She smiled and I'd never seen anything more beautiful. "Let's go."

Hand in hand, we met Paul then sprinted behind him down several hallways to an exit that led to a grassy area where carnival game booths were set up. The area was already full of people. He radioed someone then let out a sigh of relief. "Riley and Gavin are slowly making their way here now. You didn't miss anything. They'll be coming up that path. The plan is for your sister to win at one of the booths, then he'll propose. That's what you should watch for."

I shook his hand vehemently. "Thank you, Paul. I mean that."

"You're welcome." He stepped away and faded into the

background.

As we waited, Jade looked around. "This is spectacular."

"And fitting. Riley loves carnivals. You have no idea how many times she had me try for the big bear. I'd tell her that our money was better spent on hotdogs or slushies, but she always won in the end."

Jade put an arm around me. "Because you're a softie."

I hugged her. "For a select few."

Dominic appeared beside us. "Glad you made it. I was beginning to doubt you would."

"Dominic," Jade said before I had a chance to speak. "Thank you for inviting me. I wouldn't have wanted to miss this."

He smiled. "I'm glad. You two look good together."

I met his gaze. "We *are* good together. Thank you. It means a lot to me that you made sure she was here, Dominic."

He motioned to his wife as she approached. "Abby, come meet Jade."

Abby shook Jade's hand and said it was a pleasure to meet her. When she turned to me, she said, "Riley will be so happy you're here. We all are."

"Even if you came by the slowest transportation possible," Dominic said. "I'm surprised you didn't swim over."

Lacing my hand back with Jade's, I said, "You do know that you're the reason I had to take the ferry, right? Someone closes down the airport whenever he comes to the island."

"You should have said something," Dominic growled. "Many of the guests came over by helicopter for that reason."

He really didn't see his impact on those around him. My gratitude toward him almost held my tongue, but I believed he would want to know. I decided to use an analogy. "You, Dominic, are a super-yacht dragging an anchor across coral without ever looking under the waves. You need to walk among regular people with me. If you do, I know you'll build your own buoy system."

"I prefer to fly."

Okay, maybe I needed to just say it. "I'm talking about how the airport shuts down when you arrive and depart. That forces everyone to scramble because their flights are canceled. Build yourself a private airfield. That way you won't affect other people's flights."

"I could do that." He put an arm around his wife's waist. "Why hasn't anyone suggested that?"

Abby shook her head and went red. "Dom, we've been coming for years, and I didn't even think about the impact of our presence." She made a face and said, "I was a schoolteacher. I pride myself on still being down to earth, but I guess I'm as bad as you, Dom."

His head snapped back. "As *bad* as me? Since when am I the low people measure themselves against?" He referenced Jade. "If I was so horrible, would I have flown Jade here?"

Abby gave him a hug. "Sorry, I didn't mean to say it that way. I'm just embarrassed that I also didn't think—" She froze. "Wait. Dominic Corisis, did you fly Jade up here without asking Kal if he wanted you to?"

Dominic gave his wife what I could only assume was a practiced blank stare.

I jumped in. "That's what brothers do—we watch out for each other. I was just thanking Dominic."

"He was," Dominic said to Abby.

She smiled up at him. "I give you grief, Dom, but you know I wouldn't change a thing about you. You're just lucky things worked out this time." To Jade, she said, "Would you like to meet Judy and Leonardo, our children? They're not far."

"Absolutely." Jade looked to me. "If that's okay."

I nodded, wanting her to find her own footing with this new branch of my family tree. "I'll be right here."

As I watched them go, I caught a glimpse of my mother walking with an older gentleman. His head was bent toward her. She was laughing at something he'd said and . . . flirting with him? Although she was moving slowly and likely in some pain, I'd never seen her happier. "Tell me about Hamilton."

"He's Gavin's father," Dominic said.

"I know that. Is he a good person?"

"His background check is clear. The most I could dig up on him is that his focus was all business until recently. Two funerals, both for friends of his, appears to have shaken him up. He sold his company and bought a huge property with a playground for the grandchild he's impatient for. He's upfront about wanting some."

I laughed. "My mother is the same."

"I heard he invited her to stay with him while she recovers from her next surgery."

"Hold on, my mother is *moving in* with him?"

"For now, at least." He nodded toward them. "He does seem to really care for her."

There was no denying that my mother was glowing, and Hamilton had something to do with that. "How did things go when she met you?"

Dominic's expression tightened. "It'll take time, but I don't believe she's afraid of me."

"Good." I watched her stop and say something to Hamilton. The smile they shared went a long way to reassure me. "She does look happy."

Dominic lowered his voice. "Like you, the welfare of my family matters more than anything else. It's not easy stepping back and watching someone you care about put themselves in a position where they might be hurt."

"I'll kill him if he's not good to my mother."

"I'm right there with you."

"Same with Gavin and Riley . . . she loves everyone. If he hurts her . . ."

"Not only will I bring the shovels, but the cleanup crew to erase the evidence."

I laughed, gave him a look, trying to judge how serious

he was. It was hard to say. Oddly, I felt a little better. I glanced at Dominic again. "Hey, thanks for the talk the other day. It really helped me. I've made some progress. More importantly, I'm confident that I can make it happen."

He cleared his throat. "If you want I can—"

"No." I smiled at him. "But thank you."

"You're welcome." He waved. "Your mother just spotted you. Ready to meet Hamilton?"

"I am."

We started off walking together, but when I looked to the side, Dominic was gone. My mother greeted me with a huge smile and a hug so tight I thought she might snap her arms. "Kal, you came."

Still hugging her to me, I said, "I'm sorry I didn't tell you I'd be here. I should have. I needed some time to figure things out."

She leaned back and clasped my face between both of her hands. "You're here and that's all I care about." There was such love in her eyes I couldn't doubt that she meant it.

I took her hands in mine. "So, are you going to introduce me to this boyfriend of yours?"

She blushed. "He's wonderful to me, Kal." A worried look came into her eyes. "Please try to like him."

I gave her hands a squeeze. "Mom. You deserve every bit of happiness that comes your way. If he's important to you, he'll be important to me."

Tears filled her eyes. "He's important, Kal."

I nodded. Message received.

When we stepped back from each other she turned to the man at her side. "Kal, this is Hamilton. Hamilton, this is my son, Kal."

I shook his hand firmly. He looked me in the eye and didn't flinch.

"It's nice to finally meet you," he said.

"Same," I answered. A quick glance at my mother prodded me to add, "I've heard wonderful things about you. Did you recently buy a new house?"

"I did," Hamilton said with a smile. "Bring on the grandkids."

My mother beamed at me. "I completely agree. Kal, I hope you meet someone soon. I'd love for all my grandbabies to grow up together."

Normally I would have laughed that comment off, but instead I searched the crowd until I spotted Jade. "She's right there, Mom. That's the woman for me."

My mother practically hopped with joy. "Why haven't you told me about her? What's her name? Oh, she looks so sweet."

"Her name is Jade and she's a marine biologist."

"Hamilton, that's what Kal always wanted to be." Her hand came to her mouth. "Jade. Is she the same woman who found out her fiancé—"

"Yes," I cut in. That was a memory for another time. "She lives in Florida so that's where I'll be as well. I'm done dancing. It's a little scary to be starting over, but I'm not doing it alone. She's good for me, Mom."

My mother made a pleased sound. "I'm so happy to hear this."

Hamilton added, "Sounds like you're in a good place, Kal."

I met his gaze. "I am. I finally am."

We shared a real moment when he added, "Me too. It took me a while to get there, but I finally woke up to what matters most."

"Family." My mother looked at Hamilton with . . . love?

He bent and kissed her temple.

Jade joined us then. In a rush, she said, "Riley and Gavin are coming up the path. Judy found the perfect spot to watch the proposal." To my mother, she said, "Hi, I'm Jade."

My mother shook her hand then held on to it a moment longer. "Jade, I am so happy you're here. This is Hamilton."

They shook hands as well.

"We should all go," Jade urged.

I paused to offer assistance to my mother then realized Hamilton was already guiding her to where Dominic and his family were gathered. It felt strange, but also good to see her have someone else she could rely on.

Together we walked across the grass to where Judy was frantically waving for us. When we joined them, I said, "Hi, Judy."

She hugged me. "Hi, Uncle Kal."

That also felt wonderful but would take some getting used to. I wasn't sure how to best greet Leonardo, so I let him decide. He hesitated then gave me a hug as well.

When he stood back, he said, "Thank you for letting me use your submarine until you decide if you want it."

"Leonardo," Judy said. "You're not supposed to say that. Remember what Dad said?"

"He said Kal is probably going to change his mind. That's why I can't have it. You're still considering keeping it, right, Kal?"

I was saved from answering him by the appearance of Riley and Gavin on the lawn. A crowd gathered around them. I would have stepped forward to greet her as well, but I didn't want the moment to be about me. Riley was floating on air.

Together they walked to a water gun booth. Although it was impossible to hear what they were saying, it was clear that they were a couple in love. They both bent over and shot water at targets in the booth. Across from them, two mechanical horses raced toward the finish line, neck and neck, until at the very end Riley's won.

The booth attendant handed Gavin a stuffed panda that was nearly his size. From what I could tell, the stuffed bear had a velvet ring box in its paws. Gavin fumbled with the bear, looked like he wanted Riley to hold it, then posed the bear in front of him as if it was proposing to Riley.

Riley burst out laughing, and I decided I approved of

Gavin. She said something to him that made him toss the bear to the ground behind him before taking her by the hand and holding out the ring. He then said something that had her wiping tears away and nodding.

From a closer position than we were, my mother called out, "Try for twins."

They both laughed and he slid the ring onto Riley's finger. The crowd around us erupted in applause that I joined in on as they kissed. It was a beautiful moment and everything I could have wished for Riley.

Just then Riley turned and saw me. Gavin bent to say something to her then she was sprinting toward me. I met her halfway. We hugged tightly.

"You came," she said against my chest.

"Of course I did. I'd never miss a moment like this."

With tears flowing down her cheeks, she said, "I know it wasn't easy for you to come back and some of what's going on must be confusing, but it's all good. Tell me you'll stay long enough to see how good."

I nodded. "Get back to your fiancé. I'm not going anywhere. We can catch up later."

She gave me one final hug, then bolted back to Gavin's side. My mother and Hamilton were some of the first to congratulate them. I stood back with Jade. She took my hand in hers and hugged my arm to her side. "That was beautiful."

I looked away from my sister to smile down at her. "It really was. I'm glad you were here to share it with me."

CHAPTER TWENTY-FIVE

Jade

CONSIDERING WHO WAS hosting the event, I expected it to be spectacular and it was. If your favorite carnival had a baby with the kind of restaurant that refills your water each time you take a sip—this event was like that. What took me by surprise was how friendly everyone was. I'd wondered if I would have anything in common with anyone there but had quickly been reassured. Judy was a twenty-year-old in a rush to be taken seriously as an adult. Leonardo was the sweetest little boy with a remarkable understanding of all things science. After he and I debated why NASA had begun exploring the deep ocean in hopes of unlocking the secrets to space, I told him he sounded ready to teach at the university. His huge smile had been full of the kind of pride another child might have shown after successfully doing a new trick on their bike.

Alethea had come over to greet me as well. I'd braced myself for her to ask me why I wasn't wearing one of the outfits she'd chosen for me, but she told me I looked amazing and appeared to mean it. I thanked her for all she'd done, and her answer had been a wink and a promise that she'd always be around if I needed her help again.

After she'd left, Judy had announced, "That means she likes you, and Alethea doesn't like many people."

Now that I'd experienced the same kind of welcome from Kal's mother, I was feeling much more at ease. So was Kal.

When Riley and Gavin headed our way, I was eager to meet them. My enthusiasm must have shown on my face because Riley greeted me with a hug. "Jade, I'm Riley. Dismiss whatever Kal told you about me because, between the two of us, I'm the one who is right more often."

Kal laughed. "There you go, starting crap right away." He shook hands with Gavin. "Welcome to the family."

"Thank you." Gavin smiled and put his arm around Riley. "I'm glad you came. I know it means a lot to your sister."

Kal took a deep breath. "It means as much to me to be here." He glanced at me. "This is Jade."

Gavin shook my hand as well. "I hear you were flown in Corisi style."

I smiled. "I was. It was definitely different than I'm used to."

Riley leaned forward. "It's the same for us. Even Gavin, and he didn't grow up in the neighborhood Kal and I did."

Kal shrugged. "It wasn't so bad."

In unison Kal and Riley chanted, "Missing my bike as I

go to sleep. My ride is not yours to keep. If I see you ride it by, you'll be the next one to cry." Then both laughed.

Kal glanced down at me and said, "We made that up the year we got new bikes for our birthday, and they were stolen out of the hallway of our building the first week."

Riley said, "We had two rides on them."

"Two," Kal repeated. "We never did find out who took them . . ."

"But we plotted their demise many times," Riley finished.

Kal nodded. "It's a lovely neighborhood."

Riley sighed. "It really is. A lot of good people there."

"That's the truth and it definitely prepared us for anything," Kal responded. "There are perks of not having anything. You know what we never had in that neighborhood?"

Gavin shook his head. "I have no idea."

"Pickpockets," Riley supplied with a smile.

Kal said, "You always ruin my punchlines."

"Because I can read your mind." She laughed then her expression sobered. "And you can always tell when I'm lying. I'm sorry I lied to you about seeing the Corisis. I know that put you in a tough spot with Mom."

Kal and his sister shared a long look, then he said, "And I'm sorry I wasn't ready to go on that adventure with you. You were right to want to meet them, but it took me a while to see that."

The silence that followed was a little heavy, so I asked, "Riley, do you know who Richard D'Argenson is?"

"I don't," Riley said. "But there are a lot of people here I don't know yet. Many are friends of the Corisis. Why? Who is he?"

Gavin looked around then said, "A master chef. I've eaten at his restaurants—incredible food. I didn't realize he was here. I'd definitely like to meet him."

Riley pointed toward one group of people on the far side of the lawn. "We haven't hit that section yet, but I believe they're the Andrades. Dominic talks about them a lot and has shown me a few photos of them. Our sister Nicole married Stephan Andrade. Have you met her yet, Kal?"

"No."

"Want to?" Riley was already waving a woman over.

"Sure." Kal tensed then relaxed at my side.

The couple who joined us were magazine cover polished. She was tall and lean, long, straight black hair with Kal's eyes. The man beside her carried himself like he belonged in this wealthy group, but he was also tanned as if he had an outdoor lifestyle as well.

After introductions, Nicole and Kal stepped away together for a moment to speak.

Stephan nodded toward Kal and Nicole. "It must be strange, but also kind of wonderful, to go from having one sister to two."

Riley moved closer to me. "And from one brother to

three. It does take time to get used to, but they're good people. Nicole was so warm and welcoming from the first time we met."

Stephan nodded toward his wife as he said, "It was just as strange for Nicole to hear about you and Kal. She spent many years feeling she was alone. You can't imagine how much joy finding more family brings her."

Gavin added, "I get the same sense about Dominic."

That warmed my heart to hear. "Kal needed to see all of you together."

Riley nodded. "Mom told me Kal is done with dancing and is moving down to Florida with you."

My face warmed. "That's the plan."

"He looks happier than I've seen him in a long time. I'm glad he found you."

"Me too." I met her gaze. "He loves you so much."

"I know," Riley said as she wrapped an arm around Gavin. "See, I told you it would all work out."

He rolled his eyes skyward and joked, "Is this what I'm signing up for? A lifetime of you being right?"

Riley laughed. "Is that such a bad thing?"

He kissed her cheek and said, "Not at all. The world is actually much more bearable when I look at it through your eyes."

I liked that and how Riley and Gavin were together. Remembering our side goal for the day, I asked Stephan, "Do you know Richard D'Argenson?"

"Sure," he said with an easy smile. "He's married to my cousin Maddy and he's here; would you like to meet him?"

I lowered my voice. "Kal and I would. Do you think he'd go out to dinner with us tomorrow night if we asked him to?"

Stephan shot me an apologetic smile. "When I spoke to him earlier, he said he and Maddy were flying out first thing tomorrow morning. I don't know if they have plans that can be changed."

"Oh."

My disappointment must have shown because Riley stepped closer again. "I thought you didn't know him."

"I don't." I bit my bottom lip and wrinkled my nose. If Kal wasn't still talking to Nicole I would have let him take the lead. This was his family, and I didn't want to make any waves. "Okay, if I tell you what Kal and I are trying to do you have to keep it between us. It won't have the same effect if Paul knows."

"Absolutely," Riley said in a stage whisper, and everyone shifted closer.

"What are we plotting?" Judy asked as she joined with Leonardo at her side. "Whatever it is, I'm in."

"I'm on the fence until I hear the details of the endeavor," Leonardo declared. *I love that kid.*

I hesitated. "It's not a big deal, just something nice we're trying to do for someone who has been kind to us."

"Then why are we whispering?" Judy asked.

"It's a surprise for Paul."

A grin lit her face. "I love surprises. Who's Paul?"

"Kal's butler for the weekend." I looked to Kal for help, but he was still deep in a conversation with Nicole. Taking a deep breath, I decided that although this was Kal's family, if we really did build a life together, they would be mine as well. It would be good to build my own relationship with them. "He has been so kind to us. We want to do something for him. This dress, for example, was a gift from his sister. She owns Marilyn's Closet in town. Kal's suit was also a gift from her."

Stephan looked over at Kal. "That's a nice suit."

"And your dress is stunning," Riley said.

"Marilyn made it herself. She and her mother design a lot of the clothing they sell." Sure, Marilyn might not be potential friend material for me, but I had promised to spread the word about her shop.

"*Marilyn's Closet.* Judy, you and I should check it out," Riley said.

Judy nodded. "I'm always looking for new designers. I wonder how she'd feel about working with bulletproof materials."

My eyes widened.

Leonardo leaned toward me and said, "She's not joking."

Stephan raised a hand between us. "So, back to Richard. Why are you hoping to go to dinner with him?"

I shared what Kal had told me about Paul's restaurant

and how he served his late grandmother's recipes as a way of staying close to her. "Paul told Kal he has a deep appreciation for Richard's skills as a chef. In fact, it's a dream of his to meet him. We thought if we could somehow get Paul to prepare one his grandmother's recipes and have Richard taste it—"

Riley gave me a tight hug. "I love you already. That's the most beautiful thing I've ever heard. We need to make this happen."

"It was Kal's idea," I said, hugging her back. "I just offered to help."

Tapping her chin, Judy said, "The first thing we need to do is have Paul released from work tomorrow, so he has time to prepare the meal."

Gavin said, "There is the small problem of Richard and his wife leaving tomorrow morning."

"A small wrinkle that Stephan can fix. Right Stephan?" Riley looked at her brother-in-law with absolute faith in her eyes.

"I'll see what I can do," he promised.

I said, "We'll have to tell Paul something, so he'll know to make the meal."

Kal's arms came around me from behind and he gave the side of my head a kiss. "What did I miss so far?"

I smiled back at him. "I told them about what we'd like to do for Paul and we're coming up with a plan for how to make it happen."

He hugged me tighter. "You're awesome, do you know that?"

I blushed and turned back to the group. "It can't be too many people, but do you think some of you would like to come to the dinner with us? We could tell Paul it's an engagement dinner that would be made even more special if it included one of his grandmother's dishes."

"I might cry," Leonardo said.

"This is a good thing, Leo." Judy shook her brother by the shoulder.

"I bet Paul cries," Leonard added.

Riley bent to look Leonardo in the eyes. "I bet he does, but it'll be the best kind of crying. Some tears heal."

He smiled at that.

Stephan quickly updated Nicole on what we were planning. She brought a hand to her mouth. "I love this." Then she glanced at Kal. "And that we're all doing it together."

I felt emotion roll through Kal. Later, we could talk about how the day had turned out better than he'd hoped it could, but right then I wanted him to simply savor it. In my ear, Kal whispered, "Thank you."

I turned my head and said quietly, "It was your idea, Kal."

"But you made it happen."

I hugged his arms tighter around me. "We're pretty good together."

"We sure are." To the group, he asked, "So how many

people should we tell Paul to expect?"

Judy pointed to herself then Leonardo. "We're in. Riley and Gavin. Nicole and Stephan. Richard and Maddy. The two of you."

"Mom would want to come and bring Hamilton," Riley added.

Kal interjected, "That's twelve so far."

"We should invite Mom and Dad," Leonardo said.

Judy put a hand on her hip. "If Dad comes . . ."

Kal said, "It would be perfect and mean a lot to him that we thought of him. Judy, as someone who was raised without a father, I hope you never take yours for granted. Nothing is forever. Appreciate him while you have him, or one day you'll look back and regret that you didn't."

Judy opened her mouth to say something, then snapped it shut. I felt a little bad for her, but she'd been born with so much more than most had—it didn't hurt for her to be reminded to be grateful for it.

After looking around quickly, Kal added, "And Sebastian. We need to ask him if he and his wife would like to join us. It would be nice to spend time with them before we all head home."

"That would be a photo for the wall," I said. When Kal glanced down at me, I added, "All five siblings."

"And the people we love," Kal said.

I nodded and in a soft voice repeated, "And the people we love."

CHAPTER TWENTY-SIX

Kal

THE NEXT EVENING, Jade and I drove over to Paul's restaurant ahead of everyone else to thank Paul for closing down for our private event. The guest list had gone from twelve to twenty, to the cap of the restaurant including the overflow of outdoor seating.

We parked in front of a place that looked like a private home in the front but had a side building as well as a large white tent attached. There were Adirondack chairs on the lawn leading up to the house which fit with the relaxed, but upscale island atmosphere.

Jade paused at the bottom of the stairs. "Do you think we're paying for tonight?"

"Hamilton insisted on hosting." I chuckled. "Thank God."

We shared a smile. "I should have thought of that before I started inviting everyone."

"How you did it was perfect." I gave her a slow, lingering kiss, then walked with her to the entrance of the restaurant.

"I can't believe we pulled this off," she said.

I could. With Jade at my side nothing was impossible.

We were led inside to a dining room where square tables had been pushed together into a large rectangle each with its own white tablecloth. It was a modestly decorated room with dim lighting that lent an intimacy to it. My first impression was that it felt as if we'd been invited to a friend's home to eat. I hoped Paul's grandmother's recipes were up to D'Argenson's standards.

Paul came out to meet us. His face was flushed and sweaty, but he looked happy. "Thank you for this opportunity. I really appreciate it."

And he didn't even know D'Argenson was coming.

"You're welcome. We wanted to make sure you had everything set before people arrive."

"Because you'd work the kitchen if I was short on staff?" he joked.

"I would," I said without missing a beat.

Jade added, "Me too."

Paul frowned as if he wasn't sure what to say to that. "I kept the menu limited to my grandmother's favorite dish. Of course, I've added a starter course as well as salad, cheese, and desserts for later. I'm not used to serving the same main dish to everyone, though."

"They'll love it," Jade assured him.

Paul nodded. "It's the best bouillabaisse I've ever tasted, but I might be biased. I'm sure some of those who are coming tonight have refined palates."

Kal put his arm around my waist. "You've got this, Paul. And no matter what happens, your grandmother will be smiling down, knowing you served her dish tonight. While we celebrate my sister's engagement, your grandmother will be celebrating also."

Paul blinked a few times quickly then told us to choose a seat and he'd have someone bring us champagne. Left to our own devices, Jade and I studied the seating. "What do you think?" I asked.

"Anywhere is good." Dominic and Sebastian could snag the ends of the table if they wanted. I didn't care where we sat as long as we were surrounded by family.

Jade chose two seats side by side near the center of the table. We were served champagne almost as soon as we sat. Jade raised her glass and said, "To celebrations—may we have many reasons to have them."

"I'll toast to that." I tapped my glass against hers, took a sip, then leaned forward and kissed her, enjoying the taste of champagne on her lips as well. "Is your family as crazy as mine?"

She looked down. "I really only have my grandparents."

Oh, yes, she'd told me that. "Call them," I urged on impulse.

"Now?"

"Is that crazy?" It sounded crazy once I had time to think about it. "You don't have to."

She tipped her head to one side. "Why did you suggest

it?"

I asked myself the same thing, and when the answer came to me, said, "You've told me some about them, and I remember you saying you hadn't spoken to them much. Maybe I'm riding high on how well things are going with my family right now, but I imagined having a quick video chat with them so they could see how happy you are. And how happy you make me." I frowned. "Like I said—you don't have to."

She took out her phone and started a video call. The woman who answered was probably in her late seventies, but her eyes were sparkling, and she was lovely.

"Who is this?"

Jade laughed. "Grams, it's me. You can literally see my face."

"Oh, hang on, I don't know where I put my glasses. Parker, do you have my glasses on again? He does, that stinker. Well, walk them over here. Jade wants to do that video thing with the phone." A moment later, she added, "And for God's sake put some pants on. No, give me the glasses first then go get your pants."

I was gurgling on the laughter I was holding back, especially when Jade met my gaze briefly and shrugged. I'd never met any of my grandparents, but hers sounded exactly as Riley and I used to imagine ours would be. I mouthed, "I love her."

Jade smiled. "Grams, there's someone I want you—"

"Hang on. Parker no, go get your pants first, then bring me my glasses. Jade doesn't want to see your junk. Your grandfather sat outside in the sun too long yesterday and overheated his . . . down-under. I told him to put some powder on his heat rash, but he's convinced airing it out in front of the air conditioner will clear it up faster."

I coughed at that one. Jade was holding the phone so I couldn't yet see the screen and now I understood why.

Looking from me to the phone and back, Jade seemed to be regretting the decision to call them. I shifted closer and put a hand on her leg. I wasn't looking for flash and perfection. This was real and so damn funny it made me want to fly out to meet them in person.

A male voice that I assumed belonged to her grandfather grumbled, "Fine, all covered up. And here are your glasses. If you'd stop hiding mine, I wouldn't take yours."

Jade turned the phone so we'd both be visible to her grandparents. "Grams. Gramps. There's someone I want you to meet. This is Kal."

"Are you calling to tell us you're engaged again?" her grandmother asked.

"No," Jade said quickly. "We just wanted—"

Her grandmother cut in. "You're not pregnant, are you?"

"Is she pregnant?" her grandfather asked.

"I'll never know if you keep yapping." Her grandmother moved her phone so both she and her husband were in the video shot. "Jade, can you hear me? I hope I didn't mute her."

"I can hear you, Grams. And no, I'm not pregnant."

"Me neither," I said to a completely deadpan audience.

Jade jumped back in. "I was just missing you. I'm up in New England with Kal for his sister's engagement."

Her grandmother asked, "He brought you home to his family? Already? Who is this man?"

"Kal?" her grandfather asked.

I leaned closer and smiled. "That's me. Hello, sir."

Her grandfather continued, "I may be old, but you know what that means? Life in prison means less and less to me the closer I get to the end of this ride, and you know what still has fast reflexes? My trigger finger—"

"Gramps!" Jade gasped. "He would never hurt a fly."

"Because a fly would never hurt my granddaughter. We understand each other, Kal?"

"Yes, sir."

Jade looked mortified, but I liked how protective her grandfather was of her.

"It took me time to get a little revenge on Robert, but I did and now he'll think twice before he messes with a Tremblay."

"Oh, my God, Gramps, what did you do?"

Her grandmother looked as shocked as Jade did. "Parker, tell me you didn't." She brought a hand to her forehead and shook her head. "We see Robert's car around town sometimes. Your grandfather said the next time he saw it he was going to mark it."

"You scratched his car? Gramps, you know you can get in a lot of legal trouble for that."

"Don't get yourself all in a tangle. I pissed on his driver's seat."

What?

"What?" Jade echoed my thought aloud. "No. Tell me you didn't. Did anyone see you? Would they do a DNA test for something like that?"

"Oh, I was caught doing it so don't worry about that. The police officer was really nice about it once I told him what Robert had done to my granddaughter, and then I told him the story I'd stick to would be a little dementia."

Never had I heard a more fascinating story. I needed to know. "What did the policeman do?"

"After he finished laughing his ass off, he said I was lucky he wasn't wearing his camera that day and that as far as he was concerned, he never saw anything." Her grandfather put his face so close to the camera all I could see were the white hairs of his nostrils. "See, Kal, I have a license to do as I want . . . so watch yourself."

Jade shook her head. "Grams, I don't think you should let Gramps go out alone anymore."

Her grandmother came back onto the screen and rolled her eyes. "You think that would stop him? I'd rather not know. This is why we need to be down in Florida near you. We can share the babysitting."

Jade's eyes flew to mine, and I saw a question there that I was sad she even had to ask. "That's what family is for," I said simply, and tears filled her eyes.

Her grandmother smiled. "Kal, you seem like a nice boy. Be good to our little girl."

"I will," I promised.

The door of the restaurant opened. Riley, Gavin, Hamilton, and our mother walked in. Jade and I stood to greet them. "Grams, I have to go, people are starting to arrive," Jade said.

"Are you talking to your grandparents, Jade?" Riley asked in wonder, and I groaned. Like me, Riley would be curious, but unlike me, she lacked hesitation. She waved into the phone. "Hi! We love Jade."

"Who are *you*?" Jade's grandmother demanded.

"Riley. I'm Kal's twin sister." She pulled Gavin into view behind her. "And this is my fiancé, Gavin. We just got engaged yesterday."

"Congratulations," Jade's grandmother said. "You make a nice couple."

Riley beamed a smile. "Thank you! We just arrived at the restaurant where Jade and Kal planned an engagement celebration for us."

Jade's grandfather said, "Gavin, you want to know the secret to a happy marriage?"

Jade and I exchanged a look. Like me, she probably had no idea what he'd say. There was no stopping that train, though.

"Absolutely, sir," Gavin answered politely.

"Only make vows you intend to keep. If you say for better or for worse, you hang on tight through the worse. If you say you'll treasure her, never let her know when you start tuning her out. Women like to be listened to."

Gavin nodded. "Sound advice. I'll remember that."

"And one more thing," Jade's grandfather said. "Every single night . . . before you go to sleep . . . you get down on your knees . . ."

Jade made a grab for the phone, but Riley held tight. I couldn't blame her. Even I wanted to hear where this was going.

". . . and thank God he sent you someone patient enough to put up with you, because chances are she's tuning you out just as much and that's her gift to you."

Jade collapsed back against me. I chuckled and said in her ear, "Even if that had gone in an entirely different direction, Riley would still love him. She's always wanted grandparents. We both did. For her, this is like you're letting her celebrate with yours. Look how happy she is."

Jade turned to meet my gaze. "The older they get the less I know what they'll say." Just above a whisper she added, "He pissed in Robert's car."

"I can't say I disapprove."

Jade's eyes rounded.

I added, "It's a guy thing."

"Is it, though?" She didn't look convinced.

I looked up from her to see that Riley had passed Jade's phone to my mother and it was my turn to be mortified. My family was nuts. "Jade, my mother is now talking to your grandparents."

Jade's head whipped around. We both watched in silent horror as my mother held up the phone to Nicole and Stephan as they came in and said, "This is Nicole and Stephan. Nicole is Kal's other sister." Nicole looked so happy with that introduction she verged on tears. "Nicole, would you like to meet Jade's grandparents? They couldn't come today, but hopefully they'll join us for Kal and Jade's engagement party."

"I would love to," Nicole said. "Isn't technology wonderful? You couldn't be here, but with video it's almost as if you are." She laughed. "Well, thank you for that. I make sure Stephan is wearing pants whenever we head out into public too."

Jade turned and wrapped her arms around me. "Your family is so nice."

I kissed her forehead. "So is yours. And they're hilarious."

The door of the restaurant opened again. As Dominic entered with Abby and their children, Nicole held up the phone toward her brother. "Dom, Jade's grandparents couldn't make it, but they're on the phone; would you like to meet them?"

Dominic took the phone, greeted them, then pulled his wife closer so she could do more of the speaking. Abby introduced Judy and Leonardo then said she was enjoying getting to know Jade and what a great couple Jade and I were.

As soon as the door opened again, Dominic handed the phone off to Sebastian and his wife. I looked down at Jade. "We have completely lost control of this situation."

She hugged me tighter. "Why doesn't that seem as bad as it should?"

"Because we're together?" I murmured against her hair.

"Or we're both clinically insane. I prefer your theory."

CHAPTER TWENTY-SEVEN

Jade

A SHORT TIME later everyone including Richard D'Argenson and his wife, Maddy, were seated. I'd finally snatched my phone back and told my grandparents I'd call them the next day. They'd both been smiling when we ended the call and that brought another layer of magic to the evening.

When Richard entered with his wife, they chose the empty seats across from us. Stephan had introduced us briefly the night before. They'd graciously accepted our invitation to join us for the engagement party. When we'd said the restaurant was owned by a friend of ours, Maddy had said her husband was quite opinionated when it came to food. Kal suggested that we not tell Richard more than that our friend admired him. That was a gamble, though. We hadn't tasted Paul's food yet. It might be horrible. What would Richard say then?

I leaned over and whispered to Kal. "This is going to work out, right? I didn't consider how it might crush Paul if his idol doesn't like the dish."

He whispered back, "I'd want the truth."

"Should we say something? Make sure Richard softens his opinion?"

"It won't mean anything then."

I nodded. *True.* Still my stomach was in knots.

Conversation was light and easy as the waitstaff began to bring out salad plates of chicory, fennel, radishes, and toasted hazelnuts. I tried not to be obvious as I watched Richard's reaction.

He made a face at his wife. "Americans. Always the salad first. Is this a French restaurant or a restaurant that serves French food?"

Maddy hushed him. "This is a celebration, Richard, not your kitchen. Just enjoy."

He nodded and took a bite.

I shot a worried look at Kal, but he was happily talking to Sebastian about their favorite places to snorkel. *Please let Richard like Paul's food. Please.*

When the next course came, and it was only a bowl of broth I started to really worry. Beneath the table I grabbed hold of Kal's hand. He laced his fingers with mine, smiled at me, then continued his conversation with Sebastian.

I couldn't look away from Richard. He lifted his spoon, dipped it into the broth, brought it to his nose and sniffed it before taking a taste. I held my breath and waited.

He nodded once. "Now this is not bad."

I let out a relieved breath and tried the broth myself. It

was delicious. There was a definite fish taste to it, but I also recognized saffron in the tomato broth and an orange zest. When Richard began to spoon croutons and shredded cheese onto the broth, I did the same. Continuing to mimic him, I added a spoonful of a sauce that I soon discovered was spicier than I'd expected. Deliciously spicy, though.

I glanced at Kal. *Like him.*

He turned and caught me looking at him. "Sorry, Sebastian was telling me about his family. He'd like to have us visit them. Would you go with me?"

"I'd love to."

Another course arrived. This time the bowl was filled with an assortment of fish and shellfish with only a thin pool of broth beneath it. Richard dug into it without comment. Since the soup had come with both a fork and a spoon, I watched which he chose for what and did the same.

I tapped Kal's thigh, leaned over, and said to him, "I can't tell if Richard likes the food."

Kal looked across the table and said, "Richard, what do you think of the soup?"

"This is not *soup.*" He threw his hands up in the air. "This is the best bouillabaisse I have tasted in my entire life. *The best.* And I make the dish. The chef has added an ingredient so subtle I can't quite figure out what it is."

A grandmother's love. The words came to my mind, and I blinked back tears. It was probably something simple like a rare pepper, but that's not what my heart told me.

To one of the waitstaff, Richard said, "I need to speak to the chef."

A moment later, a somewhat frazzled Paul emerged from the kitchen. When he saw who had summoned him, he froze. For a moment I thought he might turn around and head back into the kitchen. He took a breath, smiled, and approached Richard. "Chef D'Argenson. I heard you'd like to speak to me."

"Yes," Richard said, as he removed his napkin from his lap, placed it on the table and stood. "This is the best bouillabaisse I have ever tasted, and I don't give compliments lightly. Is it your inspiration or someone else's?"

Paul was glowing as he said, "It's my grandmother's. She taught it to me and we would make it together whenever she would visit. This was her favorite dish and whenever I make it, I feel her with me."

Richard's face tightened then he said, "A grandmother's love. That's the ingredient that sets it apart. Intangible. Impossible to recreate. Perfection."

"Thank you, Chef D'Argenson. It is an honor to have you enjoy it."

Richard shrugged. "If it is okay with you, I will ensure I'm not the only one who will. Whenever bouillabaisse is mentioned, I will tell them there is only one place I would recommend and that is right here. I myself will return to enjoy it again. It reminds me of home."

"Thank you."

I turned to Kal and hugged his arm. "He loves it."

Kal smiled. "We did good."

"We sure did."

"Ready to go home tonight?"

Home. Florida felt like that to me now—and so did Kal. "I am." Then to lighten the mood, I added, "How about *after* dessert?"

CHAPTER TWENTY-EIGHT

Kal

A FEW MONTHS later, seated on the couch with Jade asleep next to me, I turned off the television and picked up my phone. As soon as we'd returned to Florida, I'd gotten a job at a local gym to help pay the bills. With Jade at my side, I found the courage to finally call Sal and ask him how everyone at the old gym was. He was happier to hear from me than I'd expected him to be and that was humbling. My stubborn pride had cost me a lot over the years, but I was determined to not let it guide my actions again. I promised to bring Jade up to meet him soon then Sal passed the phone to some of the men I'd known most of my life. They asked a ton of questions. I told them the tangents my life had taken before landing me in Florida with a good woman and what I hoped was a solid plan. I'd made mistakes, let too much time pass without trying to make amends, but we started fresh that day and it felt good—so good.

I was still reaching out to production companies, but Netflix hadn't called and so far, I hadn't gotten past pitching my idea for a documentary. Meanwhile, Jade and I started volunteering every weekend together and filming it with our cameras. We bought some cheap equipment and began to film our dives as well. Our focus was to raise awareness of worthwhile environmental projects and encourage donations for them.

We posted those videos on our social media platforms and at first that hadn't seemed like a wise choice. Videos of me on stage appeared on every post, often with a landslide of ridicule. Jade and I talked about the possibility of pulling the videos down but decided to face the trolls together.

We went live on one platform and brought up my dancing past. I told them that caring about the future of the planet doesn't require a particular moral standing. I'd done plenty of things I wasn't proud of. Videos of private moments at wild parties would probably continue to surface. Those mistakes would always be a part of me. So? Are people not allowed to evolve? Are we never able to be more than we were at our weakest moments? Is that what humanity has become?

Jade addressed those who mocked my lack of formal education in the field. She handled it with so much dignity and class those trolls fell silent. When she said that anyone who thinks an education can only happen in a classroom is either a fool or really a fool, I laughed. So did many of the people watching the video.

Steadily over the last couple of months she and I had built up a following for our videos. People had stopped asking me to take off my wetsuit and embarrassing video footage stopped appearing on our posts. More and more, invitations from well-known marine biologists would appear in the comments and we'd follow up on them.

With Jade snoring away beside me, I checked on the stats of our latest video. Three million views? That wasn't possible. I checked the other videos. Same and rising. It was insane. I slapped Jade's ass. "Look at this."

She groaned and blinked. "What?"

I showed her the phone. "Can those views be right?"

"Holy shit." She sat up. "Did you do something different?"

"No. You?"

"No." She opened the app on her phone. "This is crazy. Look at the comments coming in. They love you."

"Us."

"I don't understand. What changed?"

I did a search of my name online and what popped up was a quote that Jade and I were Aquaman's favorite real-life heroes. I read the quote to Jade then found his post where Jason Momoa said he'd learned my name first when I'd stolen one of his suits but forgave me when he saw all the good work I was doing for the environment. He recommended our videos to anyone who hadn't seen them as both educational and damn entertaining.

His post had been shared by several other big entertainers who agreed that Jade and I were some of their favorite influencers. Influencers? Is that what we'd become?

"Jade, my DMs are filling up."

"Mine too."

I checked. "Some of these are from sponsors."

Jade snuggled closer with her phone. "What do we do? Should we answer them? I've never dealt with something like this."

"Me neither." I took a deep breath. "We should—"

"Ask Dominic," she finished.

We both nodded.

I would never feel comfortable accepting money from him, but advice? Absolutely. Since Riley's engagement, we'd kept in touch, speaking a few times each week. I hit his number. As soon as he answered, I said, "Dom, you know those videos Jade and I post?"

"Yes."

"They've gone viral and sponsor offers are coming in. If you have time we'd like to—"

"I'm on my way," he said and ended the call.

I laughed and hugged Jade. "I was going to read a few of the messages to him to see what he thought we should do, but he's coming here."

Jade smiled. "He never does anything halfway."

"It's not a bad way to live." Right then I decided that I'd take a page out of Dominic's book and use his visit to plan something else as well. It was time to take my relationship with Jade to the next level.

CHAPTER TWENTY-NINE

Jade

Two weeks later

K AL'S PERMA-SMILE AS we packed our gear for a dive was a giveaway that there was more going on that day, but I was determined to look surprised. Kal was many things— subtle wasn't one of them.

He'd outright asked me what my ring size was then tried to pass off the question as idle curiosity. I'd caught him on the phone more than once with Sasha and Nikki. After Robert, that might have caused me some concern, but they were three-way calls that both of my friends told me I needed to pretend I hadn't overheard part of.

Whatever Kal was planning for that day required significant time and effort, so I already loved it. After Dominic had helped us sort through the messages from sponsors and choose which ones made the most sense for us to work with, Kal had gone out with him for a drink. I'd thought it was odd for Kal not to include me, but it also made sense that he might want some time alone with his brother. It was his huge grin and tender kiss when he returned that had me

283

thinking that our future might have been the topic of their talk.

My suspicion was confirmed when we'd visited my grandparents at their new condo a town over from us. He and my grandfather had gone out onto the balcony and closed the sliding glass door behind them. Their talk had ended with my grandfather smiling and giving Kal a back smacking hug.

Still smiling about that day, I walked across our living room and lifted two photos off the mantel of the fireplace. They were both from the night we celebrated Riley and Gavin's engagement. One was Sebastian, Dominic, Nicole, Kal, and Riley standing together. Of the two, this photo looked more strained and forced. The next photo was all five of them with their partners. Everyone, including me, had been caught in some stage of laughter . . . either holding some in, outright laughing, or smiling right afterward.

The reason? When we'd lined up, we'd asked one of the waitstaff if she'd take the photo. She'd agreed and kept saying how exciting it was to take the photo of someone so famous. Sebastian, Dominic, Stephan and even Gavin had stood a little straighter and puffed out their chests with pride. When the girl asked, "Could I take a photo for myself as well? No one will believe I met Invio in person. We tried to see your show the last time we were in Vegas, but it was booked solid."

When all four of the other men had looked at Kal in

surprise, the women had burst out laughing. Kal made a joke about it not being his fault he was younger and better known, then laughed and everyone else joined in. It was my favorite photo because it held a promise that no matter how they'd started off, they were now a family.

And I was part of it.

"Ready?" Kal asked from across the room.

"You're bringing luggage as well?" I asked as I noted the additional case he had in his hand. "To a dive?"

He shrugged. "We might want to go to dinner afterward. Doesn't hurt to have a change of clothing."

I nodded as if that made perfect sense. Normally we stuffed additional clothing in a backpack, but okay.

We hopped in our car and headed to the airport where the company had arranged for a sky taxi to take us down to Key West. One of our sponsors had requested we participate in a debris cleanup project just offshore while wearing their high-end BCD vests. Since friends of ours were involved in the cleanup, we'd negotiated for the company to match our fee with a donation to the project.

Kal and I still contained our paid dives to the weekends, but we were doing so well with them that I could envision us leaving our day jobs soon and working for ourselves. We chatted on and off on the trip down. I tried to read a book on my phone but every time I glanced at Kal he was smiling and that kept sending butterflies through me.

The dive itself started off pretty routine. We met up with

a team, had a few laughs with the ones we'd gotten to know well from previous dives, and walked our cameraman through what we'd like filmed. The location we'd chosen had a mostly sandy bottom so the debris would stand out and hopefully make for some powerful images.

Once in the water, we got to work cutting free or simply picking up and swimming to the surface with common but detrimental debris—discarded hook and line fishing gear and rope from old lobster traps. The team, along with recreational volunteer divers, had already removed nearly twenty thousand pounds from the area. It was a thrill to be included in the effort, profitable to be sponsored to help them, and personally satisfying to know the project would receive additional funds because of our involvement.

Kal swam ahead and disappeared behind a coral reef. A few minutes later he was back and motioning me to see something he'd discovered. I joined him, not sure what to expect. There in the sand, lines of stones were organized into a question: *Jade, will you marry me?*

I nodded then motioned for us to go to the surface. We held hands as we ascended. As soon as we broke the surface, we both took out our mouth pieces, pushed the goggles down around our necks, and kissed. I don't know how many times I said yes between those kisses, but it was enough that we both started laughing.

We swam to the boat then hopped onto the ramp, turned, and sat. Our cameraman swam up and started taking photos of us sitting together, with our legs still dangling into the water.

Kal glanced back at the pile of trash we'd removed from the sea floor. "Do you care that our engagement photo will have that as a backdrop?"

I hugged him tightly. "Are you kidding? It's perfect. I can't imagine a better background. In fact, I think we should make sure we take a photo of us on every anniversary in front of something we've done to make the world a better place."

He searched my face. "There's something I should tell you."

I no longer worried when he said that. "Yes?"

"Dominic and my mother organized a party for us tonight. He has that damn super-yacht buoyed off the coast and Judy warned me he intends to give it to you as an engagement present. You, not me, because he knows I won't accept it."

I reached out and took his hand in mine. "Is there a way to warn him ahead of time that I won't either? I don't want to embarrass him."

"Riley suggested we accept it and lend it out to research projects when we aren't filming from it. Sebastian crunched numbers and the cost of owning it would be offset by the tax benefit of donating the use of it."

"So, I should accept it?"

"I don't know. On one hand Dominic wants us to have it. On the other hand, can you really imagine us traveling the world on our own research vessel, submarine and all?"

I could. "We'd have to stay based in Florida. We should be around for my grandparents when they need us."

"Is this crazy?"

"A little, but we could do a lot of good with it."

He put an arm around me. "Crazy doesn't feel wrong at all when we choose it together."

It sure didn't. We kissed then smiled into the camera again for what will always be my favorite engagement photo of Kal and me because he said together, and I said yes.

THE END

Made in the USA
Columbia, SC
21 April 2022

59268867R00163